First Edition, May 2024

For more information, or to book an event, contact :
studio@audioverse.club
www.audioverse.club
Book design by: Urszula Postek
Cover design by: Urszula Postek

ISBN – Paperback: 9788397154308

U.E
.P.

URSZULA EDEN PUBLISHING

The SOL of Shadows

Vol.1

Tales from a Twisted Universe

Uncover the dark echoes that bind their lives in this mind-bending collection.

Parvin Romaine Rosario

CONTENTS

The SOL of Shadows / Vol.1

I. Junior's First Kill   **14**

II. Peeping Tom   **81**

III. Mailman Michael   **142**

TO GOD,

I love you so much, thank you for everything you ever done for me. Please forgive me for all my sins and the sins that will happen to me. I truly love you so so so so so much. Thank you for everything. This book is dedicated to You, the guiding force in my life. The almighty. Through every twist and turn, every triumph and tribulation, it is Your unwavering presence and boundless love that has pulled me through. You have been my anchor, my source of strength, and my solace in times of need. To You, I offer my deepest gratitude and praise.

To all the past experiences and relationships,
This book is also dedicated to all the moments and connections and people that have shaped my journey. Each encounter, whether joyful or challenging, has left

an indelible mark upon my soul. It is through these experiences and relationships that I have grown, learned, and discovered the stories and tales that now lie before you.

May the light of understanding and compassion shine upon you as you embark on this literary adventure. May the wisdom gained from past experiences illuminate your path and guide you to a future filled with goodness and fortune.

With heartfelt appreciation,

Mucho,
The Nightwriter

| ABOUT THE STORY

In the shimmering twilight of reality and illusion, three lives are about to intersect in ways that defy understanding. Each trapped in their maze of choices, they are hurtled toward destinies that intertwine the fabric of their realities into a tapestry of triumph and tragedy.

Our first protagonist, a young soldier forged in the crucible of war, is haunted by the spectres of the battlefield. Yet, it is not the physical war that wounds him most, but the emotional one. Love lost and loyalty betrayed, he is left with a heart ravaged by the scars of deceit and the phantom of an enemy he was forced to destroy. Will he find the strength to conquer the battle within, or will the toll of war consume him?

In the glossy, seductive world of technology, a reluctant participant is caught in the virtual spider's web. A man named Adam, staunchly opposed to the allure of the digital world, succumbs to its hypnotic pull. He navigates a reality where the line between the virtual and physical is blurred, a reality where the human connection becomes a pixelated illusion. Will he save his newfound friend from the snares of social media, or will he become a victim of this bewitching mirage?

Finally, we glimpse into the life of a man wrestling with the darkest corners of his psyche. A mailman, a seemingly ordinary figure in society, harbors a chilling secret — he is a serial killer. But the arrival of a woman, an embodiment of hope and redemption, triggers a struggle within him. Torn between his violent desires and a yearning for salvation, will he embrace the possibility of change, or succumb to the consuming darkness within?

"The SOL of Shadows" is an exploration of the human condition, a journey through the shifting sands of moral ambiguity. As you turn each page, you will be drawn into the depths of love and loss, deception and redemption, fear and courage. Prepare yourself for an odyssey that transcends the boundaries of the mind, pushing the limits of perception and reality. These stories are a testament to our resilience, a testament to the light that flickers even in the heart of shadows.

Welcome Dear Reader,

to a world where everything is not as it seems,

a place found in dreams

or other times in Nightmares...

I.

JUNIOR'S FIRST KILL

CHAPTER ONE

"Junior, wake up".

That's what I used to hear when I was a young kid. Waiting on it like an alarm clock from an angel in the form of my mother's voice. I knew that breakfast followed close after and my stomach could already feel the warm pancakes stretching my belly button to its limit. But this voice sounded different. I wake up to a more rugged sound of a voice. It's not my mother's like when I was a kid. Like I said back then, her call was like an angelic alarm clock announcing that a warm breakfast was on the way. But the voice that breaks through my sleep now is sharp, urgent and nothing like my mom's.

"JUNIOR, WAKE UP!" a young soldier assigned as my battle buddy yells panicking. It's my first day in basic training for the U.S Army and I overslept. Reveille music plays in the background struggling to rise above the commotion as I tossed on my uniform.

"Everyone better be outta their bunks and have their bed dress-right-dress," the Drill Sergeant roars. He's a towering figure, brown round circle hat, eyes that see everything and miss nothing, and a voice that could shatter glass. My reality is different now then back in texas. Now its bunk beds, three meals at the DFAC, and push-ups, Lots of push-ups. And you know what? I'm loving it. The military training is tough, but it's also rewarding. It feels like it's giving me back the love I'm putting into it. As the weeks went by I could tell I was excelling past my peers and the next week would be my favorite of all, rifle week.

"Get ready for the shooting range, privates!" Drill Sergeant announces. We all got loaded into the backs of big military trucks and drove out to the range to shoot. Weapons, bullet proof vests and helmets, the whole git up just like the movies.

The sound of gunfire as we arrive instantly reminds me of home. The first blast at the range takes me back. The scent of gunpowder like a time machine, bringing me straight to hunting trips with my dad in Texas where I grew up.

As a young kid I'd pester my dad about deer hunting, I remember Dad would caution me: "With all that yelling, they'll hear us coming a mile away son.'"

Drill Sergeant's voice pulls me back to reality. "Focus, Private!"

I'm eager, probably too eager and I blurt out, "I don't

miss." "Well I don't give a damn!" the drill sergeant responds humor lining his stern face. "Fantastic! Now hit that target before I rip your arm off and use it as a toothpick."

His words are always hilariously intimidating. I find it funny and sometimes I think I even egg them on just to hear what outrageous thing the drill sergeants will say next.

I lay down and peer through the sights of my M4 rifle, it's like another layer of reality overlays itself on this one. I'm back with my dad again on the day of my first big hunt.

"Don't aim at what you can't hit," my dad would say. "And don't shoot at what you can't kill," I would finish for him.

That's when I saw that deer that I shot with my dad once. My first big buck and my first deer all together. I remember my dad's face when I tracked it, we saw it looking away from us right across the field in the perfect spot. It was staring away at the horizon looking strong as jailhouse bars and more peaceful than a sunset on a private beach in Puerto Rico. I almost didn't want to kill it, but the look in my dad's eyes told me it was the key to his happiness and the password to crack the code to manhood. Killing it felt like a rite of passage, a nod from my dad that said, "You're a man now."

I pulled the trigger in what felt like a slow-motion gunshot and the deer took off running.

"I hit it dad! I really did! I hit it" My young self-held up the rifle in celebration. My dad looked on with joy and with the biggest smile he said "Great, now let's track it."

"Scan your lane!" Drill Sergeant shouts, snapping me back to the present and tearing me from my daydream. And just like that, I'm not a kid in Texas anymore. I'm a soldier in training, miles away from home, but carrying every lesson I've learned with me. And as I pull the trigger, hitting the target dead-on, I know some things never change.

As the 50-meter target appeared, my instincts took over. Boom! Target at 50 meters—down. Boom! 150 meters—gone. At 300 meters, I remembered to aim slightly above center mass then—Bang! Target neutralized. Man, I was on fire. I set my rifle down feeling like the champion of the army.

"Cease fire! Cease fire!" Drill Sergeant's voice cuts through the air. I head back to the tower joining the lineup as scores get called out. "Junior, 39 out of 40." I'm stunned. 39? How'd I miss one?

"Wait, no way! Which one did I miss?" I ask, my mind racing to figure it out.

"Who the hell you talking to private?!"

He switches back in Drill Sergeant mode. I couldn't help but start to reflect in the moment—damn, I must've missed one while lost in the memory of that deer. That creature had been so mystical, so majestic. My dad's pride when I took the shot his smile radiating warmth, filled me with an indescribable happiness.

I remember when he took the picture of me holding its rack, he wrote on it, "Juniors first kill". That day I learned there's nothing that makes a young boy more happy then the love from your mother and your fathers approval."

That was a day of love, a day of firsts, a day that made a young boy happier than he'd ever been. And just like then, I know I'm still that kid—still chasing the high of making those I love proud, still loving the discipline and the challenge, still ready to take my best shot when it counts. I finished the whole basic training with honors, top of my class to be exact, it came with special perks like leading my class in a creed we would recite in front of all the families on stage, my dad would have been so proud of me.

| *CHAPTER TWO*

Walking off that graduation stage, my chest swelled with pride from the honors pinned to me. Getting recognized in front of everyone? Man, it was like I'd dunked the final basket in a championship game. Sure, my parents weren't there, they had passed away years ago, but I felt them. They were there in spirit, somewhere in the applause and cheering.

Enter Jennifer or as I called her Jendi. My sunshine. Barely clearing five feet, she zips through the crowd and practically flies into my arms. We had known each other for a while back in texas and after a crazy night partying right before I left for the army we made it official.

"So, you think you're some big shot army guy now huh?" Jendi teased. Her voice, tinged with a London accent, as we walked together to her car.

"Top of my class," I shot back, grinning.

"So, none of those 'barely graduated high school jokes anymore." I playfully squeezed her tight, both of us holding each other as we walked.

"Fine, Mr. American Man. Where are we eating then?" Jendi's eyes flicked to mine, catching the sunlight just so. It was a sight to behold.

See Jendi possessed an aura that was almost magnetic, heavenly even. She was London-bred until high school where we met, and let me tell you, the girl knew how to make an entrance. Her blonde hair, not just any shade but a warm honey blonde, cascaded in soft, curling waves framing her face, as if meticulously crafted by an artist. Her sky-blue eyes had an innocent glow in them, reminiscent of the sun rising over a still lake—a brilliance that whispered promises of new beginnings every time our eyes met. She seemed to introduce me to an unseen world, a realm I had always been searching for but had never managed to find.

Not a towering figure by any means—rather petite in fact—but her physique more than compensated. It's as if she'd been sculpted to challenge society's beauty ideals. Her curvy posterior and artful breasts, thanks to surgical enhancements, weren't mere ornaments but rather armors against her deeper insecurities. Jendi had that girl-next-door allure—dangerous because she knew its power, doubly dangerous because she didn't overuse it.

Yet, Jendi was so much more than the sum of her

physical attributes. The girl was valedictorian, okay? And never missed an oppourtuny to tell you. She had a brain that could run circles around most people, which made her even more of an enigma. Men—and some women too—were hooked, itching to decode the riddle that she was. And she thrived in that mystery, in the uncertainty of her own narrative. Adventurous to the bone, Jendi was the type to love the wind slicing through her hair as she zoomed down a forgotten highway. She found ecstasy in the wildest situations like skydiving, but a meal from a mom-and-pop eatery in the middle of nowhere could still excite her like a child on Christmas morning.

Yet, underneath that spirited exterior lay fragments of a broken soul, wrestling with the age-old dilemma of settling down versus living wild and free.

Intelligent and attention-loving, her dual nature was her biggest paradox. She had the smarts to dissect classical literature and the charisma to light up a room just by walking in. She was that potent mix of beauty and brains, yet her love for attention could sometimes be her Achilles' heel.

Her smile, oh that smile—could light up even the darkest pits of space, illuminating my world like a supernova in the night sky.

"Junior, I'm starving. Let's eat!" She urged, pulling me out of the trance I was in. Just looking at her made me realize how much I'd missed her throughout training.

Before I knew it our lips collided. The pent-up longing, all the missed time—it just exploded.

"I missed you so much," she whispered. "Don't ever leave me again. I need you Junior."

That was it. That sealed our future together. Time seemed to fold in on itself and before I knew it, Jendi and I were sharing a home in Fort Riley, Kansas—the home of the Big Red One. I was a proud Big Red One Soldier, I wore that Big Red One title like a second skin. Mornings were a symphony of cadence calls, my voice joining the chorus of my comrades, all of us standing tall, tan boots meeting the earth in rhythmic unity.

Jendi, embraced this life like a natural, almost as if her past in London had been a prelude to this very moment. She excelled in the new routines, the joys and challenges of being a soldier's partner. Military discounts? She hunted them down with the energy of a bargain hunter on Black Friday. And when it came to supporting the troops, you'd think she was running for office. She hosted potlucks for my squad, volunteered at base events, and hung a proud 'Support Our Troops' banner right in our living room window.

In the first weeks of moving in, we had mapped out the local groceries, tested out neighborhood diners, and even found a secret scenic spot that overlooked the vast Kansas plains—our new secret getaway for when the world got too loud. We had 'our' song, 'our' movie, and a list of silly traditions that were just ours.

It was thrilling and mundane in the best way, a blend of everyday life sprinkled with the magic that was uniquely us. I loved her through and through.

But even as she nailed this role, her eyes would sometimes cloud over with worry, especially when calls from back home carried grim updates about her dad's failing health. Still she played her role to perfection, dressing up our life together like it was Sunday's best, all while juggling the weight of her family's hardships from miles away.

Towards the end of the year whispers started circling within the unit, whispers none of us wanted to admit might be true—deployment was looming. The tension was notable, gripping each of us in the unit like a vise. Finally our First Sergeant broke the uneasy silence with news that tightened that vise even more.

"Gentlemen, nothing is confirmed yet but it looks like we might be heading for a training rotation soon. And that might swiftly transition into a deployment. So I want everyone to pack their bags. We could be off to NTC in California, and let me tell you, it's brutal. No phones, no distractions. Be prepared for thirty days."

His words hung heavy in the air, like a guillotine blade poised to fall. I thought of Jendi and how she was already balancing on the edge with her father's illness. She couldn't handle much more, not now. I made up my mind then—until it was confirmed, until I had no other option but to shatter our fragile peace. I would keep this looming possibility from her. After all, some burdens are too heavy to be shared prematurely, even by those bound together as tightly as we were.

CHAPTER THREE

I would be lying if I didn't say the announcement felt like a sledgehammer to my body. This wasn't just another training, it was a prelude to what lay ahead and I knew this could make or break our relationship. A 30-day absence that could stretch the already frayed fabric of our bond to its breaking point. And if the deployment rumors were true, I'd be away for a whole year. How could our new relationship withstand that?

As if the universe were playing a cruel joke on us, tragedy struck Jendi's family. Her father got diagnosed with cancer. Looking into her eyes, I saw fragments of the strong, joyful woman I loved crumbling away. She was losing a part of herself, and the worst part? I couldn't be there to catch the falling pieces.

It was as if life looked at our struggles and said, "You think this is bad? Hold my beer."

Now I was torn between my duty to my country and my obligation to the woman I loved, a mental and emotional tug-of-war that left me reeling. Jendi needed me now more than ever and I was about to vanish into a training abyss with no contact to the outside world. The timing couldn't have been worse. Lying beside Jendi while watching a movie, we clung to each other like two lifebuoys adrift in a wave crazed ocean. I was keenly aware of the news I had yet to share, and as we huddled together in that fragile bubble of normalcy, I couldn't help but ponder: How much more could either of us take before something gave?

As if sensing the chaotic screams of my thoughts, she turned to me and asked, "Is everything okay, Junior?" The words caught in my throat, a lump of unsaid truths and unshared fears. For a fleeting moment, I considered spilling everything right then and there, but I hesitated. Instead, I chose to preserve that fragile cocoon of peace we were wrapped in, if only for a little while longer.

"Everything's fine," I whispered, sparing her the added weight of worry until I had confirmation of what lay ahead for us.

And so, I held her tighter, as if my arms could somehow shield her from the impending complexities of life that were rushing toward us like a freight train. I had to savor this moment; it was a breather I knew neither of us might find again for a long time.

NTC—the National Training Center—was the military's ultimate proving ground. Think of it as the Olympics of armed conflict, a place where each unit is rigorously tested to the edge of its capabilities. The word around the base was that this was the final hurdle before we got deployed to a much less hospitable environment. Finally the day came when the murmurs crystallized into a definite announcement. Our unit was going to be deployed, the commander confirmed it, laying out a timeline that felt both too soon and not soon enough. Training for 30 days at NTC, then a brief period back home, before shipping out for a deployment to Afghanistan that could last God knows how long. I had to tell her now.

My heart sank as I walked through the door that evening. Jendi greeted me with a smile that didn't reach her eyes, as if she already sensed the news I was about to deliver. Sitting her down, I took a deep breath, each word heavier than the last.

"Jendi, we need to talk. I have to go away for training at NTC for 30 days. And after that... I'll be deployed."

Her eyes widened, and for a moment the room was thick with silence. A silence that carried the weight of unspoken fears, unshed tears, and uncertain futures. Then her eyes watered and she lunged at me, burying her face in my chest.

"Don't leave me now Junior, I need you," she sobbed, her voice muffled against my uniform.

I held her tight, as if I could somehow shield her from the torrent of emotions that were about to come crashing down on us; but I knew I couldn't. This was the life I'd signed up for, and she had become an involuntary passenger on this turbulent journey.

I hugged her like my life depended on it, knowing that was only half the equation. "Listen Yen, I'm duty-bound. But you've gotta know you're gonna be with me, right here," I pointed to my heart, "every step of the way."

She looked up at me, her eyes searching mine as if looking for an anchor in the storm that was our life. I kissed her then, a long soulful kiss that tried to say everything words couldn't.

And as she clung to me, I realized that my battles weren't going to be just against some foreign enemy in a distant land. No, the real fight would be here, at home, preserving this fragile thing called love while being torn apart by duty, time, and distance. That was the war I couldn't afford to lose. Afghanistan was no longer a subject of whispers; it was an echoing chant that reverberated through our ranks. The atmosphere was so thick, you could practically carve it like a Thanksgiving turkey.

 That same tension migrated its way into our home, setting up residence like an unwelcome houseguest. It lurked in the awkward silences that had started to punctuate our dinners, in the subtle but growing distance that crept into our conversations. The words "I love you" now had an unspoken "and come back to me safely." Every kiss, once a simple act of love, now felt like a desperate plea, an attempt to forge an emotional armor I could take with me.

Jendi tried to keep a brave face, but her eyes betrayed her. Those eyes, which I had always thought resembled the unclouded Kansas sky, were now overcast with worry and sadness.

And so it was: Jendi wrestling with the reality of her father's illness and a heartache of a profoundly personal kind. Me, facing the grim preparations for a different sort of ordeal altogether. Each of us grappling with our own forms of impending chaos and the widening gap between us, a large gap neither knew how to bridge.

The weight of it all felt like too much to bear.

How did love survive in a climate like this?

We were about to find out.

In the last days before the big training my squad leader forced me and the guys to go out together to build a bond between us. The nights leading up to the 30 day training I put more time than I should have into the camaraderie of my squad and not Jendi. To the outside eye it seemed like just crazy laughter and the clinking of beer bottles in dimly lit bars, but it was team building. These were the men I'd be standing beside in the trenches, the brothers who'd have my back when the world erupted in chaos. But as we toasted to the nights we wouldn't remember with the people we'd never forget, a small part of me couldn't help but drift elsewhere. I thought about Jendi, about how she was grappling with the upcoming training and the impending deployment as much as I was, if not more. One evening, Jendi brought up the subject holding up a piece of paper while we were sitting on our worn-out couch, her eyes dancing with a mix of excitement and nervous anticipation.

"Junior, I have the answer! Have you heard about the Netropolis tickets? They're like Willy Wonka's golden tickets but for adults!"

I chuckled, not taking her seriously.

"Yeah, I saw the SocialChat ads, the city of the future, right?

Ran by the guy who owns electric cars and rockets and the other who owns SocialChat and basically everyones social interaction altogether? Sounds like a fairy tale."

She leaned in closer, her eyes intense. "But what if it's our way out? Our fairy tale?

What if I enter the raffle and win, we could leave all of this behind, be together without the threat of war hanging over us."

I frowned, dismissing the idea instantly.

"Jendi, that's not realistic. Thousands, probably millions will enter. The odds are—"

"Long?" she interrupted.

 "So what? Even if there's a tiny chance, shouldn't we take it? What do we have to lose?"

I looked at her, torn. On one hand, I had a duty, a commitment to serve. On the other, here was the woman I loved, offering me a way out. It was a long shot but it was possibly a different kind of life entirely.

"You don't get it Jendi. I have responsibilities, obligations. I can't just chase pipe dreams."

Her face fell and I knew instantly that I'd hurt her. "So, you're saying our life together is a pipe dream?"

"That's not what I meant," I started, but she cut me off.

"You know Junior, sometimes I wonder if you ever think about us, about our future together."

I opened my mouth to reply but words escaped me. How could I explain the tug-of-war inside me, the conflict between duty and desire, the oath I'd taken, the woman I couldn't bear to leave?

Instead, I simply watched as she got up and walked away, leaving me alone with my thoughts and the heavy realization that even love had its limits. Before I knew it, I was on a plane to California on my way to NTC.

CHAPTER FOUR

In the sweltering heat of the National Training Center, I moved like a machine clad in military drab, my boots collecting the dust of this barren landscape. Each bullet I fired, each order I barked, was a dark roar—a cry for the life I had left behind, for the woman whose absence tore through me like shrapnel. If this was a preview of Afghanistan, I was in for an inferno. Nights were different. The barren desert sky unfurled like a black cloth studded with stars, and I would find myself wondering if Jendi was looking up at that same sky. Did she see Orion? The Big Dipper? The dim twinkle of far-off worlds? Did she feel the same empty void? Then after 28 days of suck came the moment we'd all been waiting for, our First Sergeant's voice cutting through the tension: "Pack up, boys! We go home in two days, great job!"

When they moved the unit to a more relaxed area it was equipped with everything you could want to buy. Food trucks all around, which was a major upgrade from the military grub we survived on for 28 days, for sure. But all I could think of was Jendi.

Back with our phones, I was hit by a barrage of notifications. Seventeen voice messages, all from her. As I played the first one, a smirk appeared on my face.

"Hey, it's lonely here… and weird without you. Dad's condition isn't helping. Come back soon?" Voice-mail: message marked for deletion.

My smirk was short-lived.

"Met some people at the park, they've been a distraction. We're dining together tonight." Voice-mail: message marked for deletion.

"Last night? Wild! Felt like I was a teen all over again. You should meet Carlos when you're back. You'd dig his vibe."

Voice-mail: message marked for deletion.

I felt a pit in my stomach.

"Hey…um, why don't you…?" followed by the sound of a kiss. A male voice, "Take it off baby, damn" Jendi, laughing, and the man blurting out "Your phone's on?" followed by her response a panicked "Is it?" Voice-mail: message marked for deletion.

The last one felt like a gut punch.

"Junior, I can't do this! I hate feeling this way. I can't handle you being gone, I've moved out… Maybe it's better if I just vanish for a while." Voice-mail: message marked for deletion. Everything around me started to blur. The noise of celebrating soldiers, the scent of food trucks, the dust in the air… it all faded away. I was surrounded by my squad, yet I felt miles away from everything. Here I was trained to face any adversity on the battlefield, but unprepared for this emotional minefield. The ache in my heart? No combat drill had trained me for that. When I arrived back home, the driveway seemed longer as I approached the house. Every step echoed with memories of Jendi's laughter, her soft touches, and whispered secrets. As I pushed open the front door, the silence was deafening. The house felt like a hollowed-out shell, a mere shadow of the home it once was. All the little things that made our house a home were now gone. Her favorite coffee mug on the kitchen counter, the scent of her lavender shampoo, the soft hum of the TV playing her favorite shows – it was all gone. The rooms seemed to echo back the raw edges of my emotions. I could see the indentations on the carpet where our furniture once was. The emptiness reminded me that it wasn't just the physical objects that were missing, but the energy, warmth, and love that Jendi brought to every corner. But there wasn't time to dwell in the past or the pain. I was a soldier first, and duty called. The deployment was imminent, and my unit was ramping up for the treacherous terrains of Afghanistan. Grief had to be set aside, tucked away like a secret letter, only to be read when the mission was over. Weeks turned into a blur as we geared up for deployment. Each morning we were up before the sun, our boots creating synchronized rhythms on the gravel, as we prepared for the unforeseen battles ahead. It was as if our training was a drug, numbing the pain of personal losses, with the relentless pursuit of readiness taking its place.

During the small break before the deployment, I sat in my now empty house missing the warm feeling of Jendi that made it a home. As my voice echoed against the walls, I had forgotten all the furniture was hers. Determined not to leave for Afghanistan without seeing her face I decided to call. My fingers trembling as I dialed Jendi's number. It was a shot in the dark, but I'd heard whispers from a mutual friend that she might have relocated to London. My heart raced with each ring, praying she'd pick up.

"Jendi... it's Junior. I need to see you. I'm asking for leave to come to London. I need to hear from you, to understand..."

With newfound resolve, I headed to Commander Thompson's tent. He was a veteran with a weathered face and eyes that had seen too much. He looked up as I approached.

"Junior, what brings you here?"

Taking a shaky breath I replied, "Sir, I'd like to request leave before our deployment. I need to go to London."

His penetrating gaze sized me up for a moment. "Is this about Jendi?"

I nodded, surprised that he knew. "Yes, sir."

He leaned back in his chair, the weight of countless

battles evident in his eyes.

"Listen son. War has a way of changing a man. But love? Love can either anchor you or tear you apart. Love isn't always about the reasons or the whys. Sometimes it's about moving forward even when everything inside you wants to look back. I can't grant your leave. We're on the brink of deployment, and every man counts."

Feeling like the wind had been knocked out of me, I murmured, "Understood, sir." The commander, in a softer tone added, "Sometimes the toughest battles we fight are not on foreign soil but within our hearts. Stay strong."

I saluted and retreated, feeling the weight of love, duty, and the war that lay ahead. With no one there to see me off the plane ride to Afghanistan was hell. I mean I understand couples don't see eye to eye but to leave a Soldier like that right before deployment, I don't think I slept for weeks. Everyday the sun got hotter and the patrols got longer. At first I thought about her so much it was a distraction, over time like everything else it faded and I got focused on each task at hand.

CHAPTER FIVE

Before I knew it there I was, 4 months into deployment standing at a rooftop lookout point stationed in Kandahar. The dusty haze below only slightly obscured the view of the village. The adrenaline coursing through my veins made the world seem sharper and every sound crisper. Doors that might conceal dangers, alleyways where threats might lurk, we sized it all up, awaiting that singular moment to pounce on a target up the road. Time felt stretched on that rooftop. Every second weighed down by the anticipation of what was about to come. The radio crackled to life intermittently with updates, but the one command we all waited for was yet to come.

And then it did. The radio's buzz sliced through the tension like a blade. Then are squad leader yelled

"Renegades, move out!"

The air was filled with this electrifying energy, then came the team's battle cry as they geared up to descend. Everybody was yelling with excitement "WOOOO!! THIS

IS IT! LET'S DO THIS!!"

Every ounce of training, every drop of sweat shed in preparation, had led us to this moment. We were ready to face whatever was up the road ahead. Or at least that's what we thought as we finally pulled out.

I gripped the handles of the .50 caliber, it's the long big gun strapped to the top of every HMMWV, "The problem solver" as we called it. My fingers started digging into the metal as the HMMWV hummed beneath me. I was responsible for the vehicle's security. Every bump on the road resonated through the soles of my boots, reminding me of the weight on my shoulders. I cast a steady gaze on my sector as our convoy of eight vehicles started advancing through the village.

Then the eerie silence made the hairs on all our arms stick up. This village had always been a mad house of bargains and yells with the cattle being sold. The streets tight with barely enough room to get the trucks through.

Now the usually bustling market that greeted us during our patrols was nothing more than a hollow memory. Stalls stood empty and the vibrant rugs that were normally laid out and showcased local pottery, lay neglected. All that remained was the haunting dance of sand and wind. A deep unease settled in my chest, reminding me of those moments before a storm hits in the country plains.

My fingers held firm on the cold metal of the .50 caliber, stationed atop the HMMWV, it was in a turret so I could move it where I needed it. I had the weight of the vehicle's safety on my shoulders, and the responsibility felt as heavy as the armor I wore.

When we drove through the village bazaar area towards our target is when the quiet really hit home. First I heard yelling, then the first burst of AK-47 fire sliced through the silence, so sudden that it took a few seconds for my brain to register the chaos. I didn't even have to turn. I saw out of the corner of my eye as Lieutenant Walters clutched at his neck, blood seeping through his fingers. Everything went silent until the frantic shouts of my squad leader filled the air, his voice thick with desperation.

 "Medic! Medic!" But even as he screamed, I could see it in his eyes, in the resigned slump of his shoulders – Walters was gone.

Rage consumed me, coursing through my veins like an electric shock. My vision blurred, the world tinting crimson. I let loose on the .50 cal, its deafening roar echoing my inner fury. Bullets rained down, carving a path of destruction on the buildings and streets. Anger passed over me like bath water. Hitting every crevice of my face and hands, I needed revenge like I needed a kidney. I saw silhouettes scramble, darting for cover as our whole convoy retaliated. Our enemy scattered – hell everyone and everything scattered – their dark silhouettes falling between doorways and alleys, desperate to escape our onslaught. And then, as abruptly as it started, a voice rang out.

"Ceasefire! I said ceasefire! Left side chill the fuck out!" The platoon sergeant yelling for his eager platoon to stop firing. After the sounds of battle were replaced by an oppressive silence, broken only by the medic's frantic pleas and the distant cries of the wounded.

After the silence settled and the dust from our retaliation settled I scanned the scene. The stark reality hit: bodies laying flat, lifeless, fathers and sons never returning home. The scene and the smell pulled my mind into a disjointed memory of my first deer hunt, another kill, my first kill.

One of my squad members starts taunting me as he checks bodies on the ground,"Hey Junior, you didn't hit shit!! Ha ha ha ha!!" As the taunts and laughter rang in the air, my world began to blur at the edges. The sounds of the battleground faded into the background as a vivid memory rushed to the front of my mind.

The texa tall grass swayed gently under a golden sun, the afternoon silence broken only by the soft crunching of boots on the undergrowth. The familiar weight of the hunting rifle rested on my shoulder, and my father's voice whispered caution in my ear.
"Junior," my father murmured, "Just keep low and

follow me. It's close and if it's not dead, it's gonna be pissed. Let's follow the drops of blood."

My young eyes, sharp and attentive, darted from spot to spot. Each drop of blood, each broken twig, was a breadcrumb on the trail of the majestic deer we were tracking.

As the blood spots got more frequent and bigger, the anticipation grew, each heartbeat echoing in my ears louder than the last. My father, sensing the proximity of my kill, whispered almost to himself, "It should be right around here. Lost a lot of blood in this spot. Maybe right around..."

The vivid memory was interrupted abruptly by my battle buddy, his voice pulling me back to the harsh reality of the war-torn village, "Hey Junior, you got one!"

For a split second, the world of hunting with my father and the present melded into one, making it difficult for me to differentiate between the two. My heart thudded loudly, the familiar rush of adrenaline reminiscent of my youth when I made a potentially successful shot during that hunt. "I got one?" I questioned, trying to ground myself.

"Behind the wall!" He clarified.

With each step toward the wall, the past and present began to blur. I could almost see myself as a young boy, eagerly rushing through the woods towards the spot where I believed my deer lay. My father's broad back just a few paces ahead, leading the way. The excitement in my younger self's eyes, seeking validation from my father, yearning for that nod of approval.

But as I approached the wall in this war-torn place, that happiness morphed into apprehension. The deer's form from my childhood memory gradually took on a more human shape. Instead of seeing my father's proud and smiling face as we approached our hunt, it transformed into my battle buddy's face, contorted with a mix of relief, disgust, and the burdens of war.

Laying behind the wall was no deer, it was a man, his clothes torn apart soaked in blood, face covered in dirt and sweat. A prominent tattoo covering his neck, perhaps a marker of his affiliation or a memory he held close. The devastation from the .50 caliber was evident, a gaping wound replacing where his life once thrived.

"How do you know it was me?" I asked, my voice almost a whisper.

My squad mate, still gazing at the man with the tattoo, responded, "Look at the size of that hole. Your .50 did that. Through the wall too. You're the only one who could cause that kinda damage. Good job, you got him."

That mixture of praise set against the cruel aftermath of war weighed on me. This wasn't like shooting a deer feeling that pride as a boy. This was someone's son, someone's father. Someone who once had dreams, memories, and a tattoo that meant something.

Someone who would never again embrace the warmth of their loved ones. My favorite squad member Nate, ever vocal, slapped my back with a loud, "Way to go, Junior!"

I turned to him, fury and pain clear in my eyes. "All these men, dead. LT could be dead, and you're cheering?"

His face fell slightly, trying to reconcile the camaraderie with the weight of the situation. "Chill out. We're brothers, Junior. We got each other."

My raw emotions overflowed."She's gone, Nate!" My voice cracked with raw emotion. "She's gone man, no more love, no more dancing, no more kisses, no more laughter.... and she is with a fucking little bitch of a man I could kill so easily!"

Nate's arms wrapped around me tightly in a calming gesture as I struggled to get free, snot and sweat dripping from my face. "Hey easy. We're here and now. Leave home at home."

But home wasn't what it used to be. The weight of taking a life, combined with my personal pain, was almost too much. Suddenly, the Platoon Sergeant's voice cut through our exchange.

"Mount up!" His words were punctuated by the grim news, "Got word from the medivac, LT didn't make it."

Expressions around me mirrored my shock. Nate, anger evident, growled, "Let's find all these motherfuckers and kill them tonight!"

But the Platoon Sergeant, ever the voice of reason, intervened.

"Calm down! Stay focused and let's be careful and get back to base."

The chorus of "hooah" that followed was more muted this time, the weight of the day pressing down on all of us. As our convoy rumbled closer to base, the passage of time felt distorted, each minute stretching to feel like hours. The weight of defeat settled on every face, every pair of eyes clouded with the stormy mix of regret, sorrow, and introspection. That ride felt like an eternity, a journey through the shared trauma of what we had witnessed and what some had done.

Upon reaching the base, the ambiance shifted. The roaring engines died down, replaced by the more familiar sounds of the camp. Soldiers dispersed, seeking relief in whatever activities they could find. Tents sprung to life with light and chatter, a stark contrast to the oppressive atmosphere of the convoy. Inside, soldiers tried to find a sliver of normalcy. The familiar sound of cards being shuffled and dealt echoed from one of the tents. Spades – a game that, for a moment, could make one forget the realities outside.

As the game went on, amidst the banter and camaraderie, a name surfaced, causing a momentary pause in the card game.

"Hey, did y'all hear about CPL DeMarco?" one soldier began, "Guy won the lottery raffle on SocialChat and left Afghanistan to head to Netropolis. Talk about a wild turn of events."

Another soldier, looking puzzled, responded, "DeMarco? I thought he was a sergeant."

"No, no," another chimed in, "You're thinking of Sgt. Carrington. But damn, Netropolis, huh? Lucky bastard."

The tent filled with a mix of envy and amusement, and just like that the tension eased a bit, if only momentarily.

"I guess Jendi was on to something" I said out loud, lighting a cigarette.

Lost in thought I sat outside, the haunting image of that man's face refusing to fade. The guilt was suffocating, each heartbeat a reminder of the life I had taken.

Nate, always observant, tried to pull me from my thoughts. He sat next to me grabbed my cigarette and took a drag "Hey man, we're protected by the scriptures!" he began, hoping to counsel.

"There's something about fighting for your homeland, for your brethren. You're on the right side, Junior."

"Killing is justified if it's for our country?" I asked myself puzzled, skepticism and hope battling within.

"Exactly!" Nate declared, his voice firm.

I wanted to believe him, to find solace in his words, I went inside and hoped that sleep would bring me some relief. Night settled around us, and the once lively tent now lay shrouded in darkness, except for the occasional rustling of a soldier in slumber. But my dreams were feverish. I felt the chilling touch of rain, the cold press of the man's head against mine like two fighters face to face before a bout, a haunting mirror of reality. In the dream, rain poured, each drop a stinging reminder of the life I had taken. I awoke gasping, my bed soaked. Was it sweat, or the rain from my dream made real?

The shrill alarm of incoming mortars snapped me to reality. The tent, a previously quiet sanctuary, erupted in chaos. Soldiers scrambled, rushing for safety. Yet, I was frozen, as though the shadow of death had already cast its cloak over me.

The Platoon sergeant's voice crackled through the commotion, "Squad leaders, report your counts!"

Dragging myself from the depths of despair, I joined my group.

Nate's voice, tinged with worry, reached my ears.

"Junior, come back to us. We have a mission."

I nodded, though inside I was drowning.

I knew he was right. But the weight of war is something no training can prepare you for. The grime, the smoke, the echoes of cries and gunshots - they imprint on your soul. Holding my rifle, it started feeling less like a tool of defense, and more like a deadly remote with a seductive promise to silence my spiraling thoughts.

CHAPTER SIX

But I couldn't let the team know what I was thinking. Hiding this darkness was essential. The guys looked to me to be their pillar, the rock they could lean on. But each night, as I tried to close my eyes, my mind was a battleground, the weight of guilt and fear a crushing force.

My dreams turned nightmarish. That same man, haunting me in my dreams. His face riding the darkest storm cloud. Some nights he'd be inches from my face, his cold breath brushing my skin. Other times he'd be lost in a bustling crowd, yet I could always sense him, I could always feel the storm he brought with him around me. One afternoon, after a mission that felt like it would never end, me and the team grabbed a forbidden moment of relaxation. My squadmate Specialist Wells, ever resourceful, had smuggled in moonshine through the mail. He grinned, handing me the bottle, and said, "Desperate times, desperate measures." Without thinking, I gulped it down. The liquid burned, each fiery sip erasing, if just for a moment, the memory of that haunting face. Wells grabbed it before I finished the bottle yelling "Give me that fool! You only need a shot of this. It's strong as hell!"

He was right. My insides felt like they were cooking but the head spinning warmth was welcomed and appreciated. That very night, the dream evolved. The man I killed told me his name was Khalid as he whispered chillingly, "You'll never be free of me, soldier." The realness of it, the feeling of his cold breath on my ear, sent shivers down my spine.

Waking up, my heart still pounding, alarms blared. Yet Khalid's voice still echoed, his presence felt in every corner of my world. Over the next weeks, it felt like he was everywhere, watching me. A shadow in the corner of my eye, a reflection in the mirror - Khalid's presence was inescapable. I felt like I was unraveling, torn between reality and the prison of my mind. What was this grip he had over me? How did I shake off this haunting shadow?

The next day the echoing call of the mail clerk pierced the ever-present hum of base camp activities.

"Junior!!! You've got mail!"

Who? Who in the world would even think of me here? It's impossible. Perhaps a mistake. But as the envelope found its way into my hands, her name caught my eye. Jendi.

Mixed emotions surged, like electricity sparking through a frayed wire. Was it happiness or anxiety?

Maybe it was resentment?

 I still felt betrayed by Jendi, yet there was an undertow of vulnerability, as if my lifeline had been cut. Perhaps it was just the vulnerability of a young soldier aching for home.

Clutching the envelope tightly, I retreated to my corner, desperately wanting to shield this fragile moment from the disorderly world outside. It carried her essence, Jendi's unique fragrance wafted up, nearly flooring me with a barrage of memories. I don't know if it was allergies or what but I read it with tears in my eyes.

Dear Junior,

I hope this letter finds you better than I am at the moment. The days here are long, and the nights are even longer. I've found myself at this little motel — a place I never imagined I'd be. The hum of the old AC and the flickering lights are the only company I've had for days.

Sometimes when I roll the window down, I catch the scent of the world outside, and it reminds me of better times. Times I often think about. Especially the moments we shared. I find comfort in the long showers here, letting the water wash over me, wishing it could wash away more than just the physical grime.

Please know, amidst all of this, my thoughts drift to you. Hoping that wherever you are, it's a place brighter than where I am now.

Love always,

Jendi

The letter's return address caught my eye — a nondescript motel called "Round up" in a place I'd never heard of. Was Jendi on the road?

Maybe she was escaping something, seeking support or comfort, or on an adventure of her own. The thought that amidst all that, she had stopped to think of me. It was both puzzling and heart-warming. What had prompted her to reach out from that unlikely place? The mysteries behind that address made her message all the more touching. Her words were like the touch of a loved one after a prolonged absence - comforting, yet filled with unsaid longing and pain. I felt a lump form in my throat, realizing she hadn't forgotten. But, there was also the guilt. Guilt of thinking she might have moved on, guilt of being mad at her.

That bubble of emotion was rudely burst by Nate's teasing voice. "Whatcha reading, Junior? Love letters in the middle of a warzone?"

He didn't wait for a response, snatching the letter away and theatrically reading her words aloud. The tent filled with laughter, each chuckle like a dagger to my already fragile heart. I snatched it back but my letter was torn in half in the process. I tried to smell it quickly but the lingering fragrance was now tainted by Nate's gritty scent. It was as if he'd stolen a piece of my soul, and in that moment, the floodgates opened. Rage, sadness, confusion – it all poured out in a firestorm of emotion. My hands reached for his neck and the next thing I knew, I was pounding on Nate, lost in a whirlwind of bloody knuckles and rage.

Stunned silence replaced the laughter. Now everyone's faces filled with shock. I could've sworn I saw Khalid from the corner of my eye, his haunting face in the crowd of soldiers grinning at my downfall.

"Enough! Get off him, Junior!" Suddenly, a pair of strong hands yanked me back slamming me against a cold metal locker. My Platoon Sergeant's eyes bore into mine, a strong concoction of anger and sorrow.

"Sixteen more days, Junior. Sixteen. And you choose now to snap?"

He said as his arms were pushing me into the locker and holding me in the air by my uniform.

I crumpled, the weight of everything crashing down.

The letter, the face of Khalid, Jendi's fragrance - it was all too much. I whispered, voice choked, "It wasn't just a letter. It was a piece of home."

I smacked his arms off me and walked away, back to my corner while the medics helped Nate.

Coming home wasn't as triumphant as the movies made it out to be. Upon return, I was singled out for mandatory sessions with the military's psychiatrist, it was part of my punishment for attacking Nate. They suspected PTSD. I stepped into those therapy rooms with the face of a poker player. Determined never to divulge the haunting reality of my now everyday sightings of Khalid, the man I had killed in Afghanistan. To share that secret could mean a fast track to a straitjacket. But as I sat on the cold leather, the weight of my silence became unbearable. My psychiatrist, Dr. Marquez, had this gift, or curse depending on how you see it, to effortlessly dig through one's mind. Over weeks she gently navigated our conversations from Jendi to possible childhood trauma, hell we even talked about the misdemeanor I caught stealing candy as a kid. Without warning she asked about Afghanistan, "Do the actions you took in battle bother you Junior?"

My voice trembled as I let out my secret: Khalid was everywhere. "Who is Khalid Junior?"

My chin sunk into my chest "He's the man I shot in Afghanistan" She started writing on her notepad. I hated that.

"How often do you see Khalid, Junior?" Dr. Marquez asked, her tone soft but probing,

"All the time," I admitted. "He started in my dreams, he came as a storm, its hard to explain. Now every crowd, every car, every face - he's there. It used to terrify me. But recently? There's been this twisted sense of companionship. He's become like my shadow."
She scribbled some more on her pad, an action she rarely took during our sessions. Panic surged within me.

"Does he ever speak to you?" she inquired, her eyes never leaving mine.

"Sometimes, and it feels so real. He has no demands, he's just always there, his energy matching mines, he rarely talks just watching, always watching me." I whispered, my voice nearly breaking.
She rips off a piece of paper with a note for me to give to her front desk. It was some kinda PTSD mood changing drug to help with my visions and anger and to all together make me whole.

CHAPTER SEVEN

I picked up my pills at the pharmacy and rushed home with them. I didn't even google the name for side effects. In the six months that went by, I had forgotten what normal felt like and I wanted it back at all costs. I grabbed the recommended dose and popped it in my mouth. Twenty minutes after I took the pills I felt nothing, and not that they didn't work. Nothing I mean I struggled to feel the breeze blowing directly in my face.

The pills transformed me. Over weeks I became a hollow version of myself. My surroundings became a blur. Nothing seemed important no matter what it was—or who it was. The world moved, but I was frozen. An irate driver honked at me, and I barely noticed. Dog shit squished under my shoe, and I didn't flinch. I was numb.

A familiar voice cut through my fog at the mall. It was Nate, traces of our brawl still visible on his face. Ashley, his wife, was beside him, eyes darting between us, curiosity evident.

"Junior, this is Tracy," Nate introduced. She smiled, though her eyes remained wary.

Nate's wife spoke, her voice gentle yet pointed. "Heard about what happened. Nate had it coming, being an idiot and all. He mentioned you two were close during deployment."

Nate's gaze deepened, "Remember that day, Junior? The day you took down that man? We found a photo of his son on him. You should've seen what your bullet did…"

I felt that familiar tightening in my chest, the walls closing in, and Khalid's eyes piercing through the crowd. I don't remember anything as I flew back to her dimly lit office in a daze, opening the door as her current patient gasped watching as desperation clawed at me. "I need a higher dose," I pleaded.

Dr. Marquez sighed deeply, walking me out by the arm. "Junior, it's not a solution. You just started-"

But my voice cracked with urgency. "Please. Anything to keep him away."

Shaking her head, she wrote a stronger prescription. The world around me grew more distant with every pill. Reality and nightmares blurred, pushing me further from everything I once knew.

I felt like I was living underwater, everything muffled, distant, and dull. The days blended together like a watercolor painting left out in the rain, with no distinct lines or features. It was like I was that lone leaf, twirling in the wind, never settling, never finding a place to call home.

Strolling back to my apartment, I figured some booze might be a decent therapy substitute. Mixing alcohol with the meds usually knocked me out cold, and sleep was now the only escape where I could still feel something. Dreamland became my haven, a sanctuary from the numbness of my reality.

Suddenly mid walk, an old, familiar scent hit me as I approached my building—a fragrance I hadn't smelled in years. It grew more potent with each step. By the time I was at my apartment on the third floor, it was unmistakable. I knew that scent, that was her scent.

When I got to my door, I noticed it wasn't fully shut. The old me might've panicked, but these meds had me on a tight leash. With a deep breath, I nudged the door open.

Jendi was there, broom in hand, back turned to me dancing and singing to herself, lost in the music from her headphones.

"Jendi?" I whispered, convinced my eyes were playing tricks on me.

The door slammed shut from a gust of wind, making her jump. She yanked her headphones off, turning around, our eyes locking onto each other's.

She looked relieved, almost as if she'd been waiting a while. "God, Junior, you scared me!"

My heart, deadened for so long, started pounding in my chest. "How... How did you get in here?"

Pulling me into a warm embrace, she whispered, "I missed you so much." Tears streamed down her cheeks. For the first time in what felt like forever, warmth spread through me. I could feel again and It was as if she was the missing piece that made me whole. The world faded as I held her tight and I was no longer numb. Each color on the wall popped with extra glow and depth. For the first time in a long time I felt grounded, not daydreaming like always, but here in reality in this embrace with Jendi.

But as I looked over her shoulder, a chill ran down my spine. There he was again. Khalid, with his icy stare, watching us.

Panicking, I staggered back, knocking into a side table. "Khalid?!"

She looked around, confused. "Who's Khalid?"

I tried to find my words, but they escaped me. "It's... It's nothing."

She gave me a worried look. "You sure? You don't look so good."

Shaking off the feeling, I asked, "how are you here?"

She gave a guilty smile, "Well, I might've borrowed your spare key under the rock outside like always... But it was only because I wanted to surprise you."

My gaze flashed to Khalid, whose anger seemed to be bubbling just beneath the surface. "Yeah, you definitely surprised me."

The weight of the silence between us grew heavy, but I finally managed to say, "I got your letter."

Her eyes widened with a mix of surprise and vulnerability. "You did?"

Khalid now looked even more angry as if he was upset. I tried not to look at him as I nodded slowly, fighting back the emotions threatening to spill over. "Reading that, Jendi... I thought you had forgotten about me. That letter felt like the lifeline I needed in that dark time."

She reached out, placing a delicate hand on mine. "I never forgot about you, Junior. Never."

But my focus kept getting pulled away by Khalid. I hadn't seen him since I started the pills and his presence loomed large in the room, like a dark cloud casting its shadow. When I locked eyes with him his were bloodshot and he was breathing fast and heavy as If he could not control his anger for much longer. I didn't know if he was mad at Jendi for hurting me or me for taking the pills and making him go away.

Jendi looked at me with concern. "You don't seem okay. You're drenched in sweat. Just... hold on." She dashed to the kitchen, leaving me with Khalid's relentless, furious stare. I couldn't keep my eyes off him; it was like I could feel his anger all through me.

As Jendi stepped towards the kitchen for a glass of water, Khalid was already there in a flash his presence dark and heavy. His breathing was harsh, like the hiss of a snake. It felt like the world had gone mute; all I could hear was my own heart thudding loudly in my ears and his breathing. She walked past him, blind to his threatening presence in the kitchen, as if she couldn't see him, and every instinct in me screamed that she was walking into danger.

Without a second thought, I lunged towards her, pulling her back from Khalid's reach, my heart racing a mile a minute.

But Jendi, mistaking my panic for something else, eased me back into the chair with a soft, "Hey, it's okay," her touch grounding me in the midst of the chaos.

She came back, offering me the water, her face etched with concern, but behind her, Khalid's rage seemed to boil over, setting the atmosphere ablaze.

"Here, drink up," she said.

Glancing at my wristwatch, I calculated the time until my next dosage. I still had four more hours, but I needed to get control of Khalid. Hastily, I fumbled in my pocket, producing two more pills.

Jendi's voice was thick with worry. "What are those?"

"I've started therapy. Everything's... it's all different now, Jendi." I swallowed hard, looking deep into her eyes.   "But where the hell were you?"

She hesitated, searching for the right words. "I was... I was reinventing myself, healing. I felt suffocated, Junior."

"But I wasn't here," I countered, frustration edging my voice, Khalid's anger so present in the room I was absorbing it.

She exhaled, looking down. "It wasn't just you. It was this life – our life. Even when you were here, you felt miles away. I had to fend for myself, find love and comfort from within because you... you were somewhere else." The room seemed to pulse with tension as Jendi's voice quivered, "I felt smothered, Junior. Lost in the shadows of your absence. I was constantly reaching out, hoping for something to hold onto. I had to fend for myself, to be my own rock, my own source of love because you were always gone."

Without thinking, the words exploded from me, "And to fill that void, you turned to fucking some guy, didn't you? I heard every word on that voicemail."

She froze, tears forming in her eyes. "You... you heard that? Oh, Junior..."

"Enough!" I snapped, cutting her off, Khalid and I standing up at the same time as if synchronized in anger. "Why are you even here?"

I shook my head disappointed, unable to bear the weight of the truth and betrayal. "Why even show up now?"

She took a deep breath, her eyes spilling over with tears, "I'm here because I still love you. Even with all the pain. Even now with–"

I shot back, raw with emotion, "I don't love you!"

I don't know why I said it but as the words left my mouth, I knew they were a lie. Deep down, love for her pulsed through every vein, but my current numbness allowed only the fiery sting of anger to break through. She gathered her belongings, casting one last, heart-wrenching glance my way.

"I returned because I love you, Junior. But I deserve respect, not resentment."

As she grabbed her things she looked back with the saddest face.

I watched, paralyzed, as she walked out, every part of me screaming to stop her. To tell her the truth.

"No, Jendi, wait! I didn't mean it!"

But I was emotionless. Now it was just me and Khalid. When Jendi left his breathing calmed down but why was he here I took my medication. Why did I take those stupid extra pills, And let her leave.

CHAPTER EIGHT

I wish I could scream out for Jendi. I cursed myself for gulping down those extra pills and letting her slip through my fingers. Now everyone was gone. Except for Khalid. There he was, his stalking presence thickening the air. Why was he still here? I took my medication. In a fit of frustration and desperation, I flung the pill bottle across the room.

The following days were a blur, each moment stretching endlessly. After tossing the pill bottle in the trash, I spent the following days in a frenzy. The numbness I felt on those pills made it so I couldn't feel anything for anyone, not even for Jendi. But as soon as she left I wanted to find her, to say "I'm sorry" and explain the pills. The city stretched before me, a puzzling world of possibilities. Each step was fueled by a desperation I could hardly contain. Khalid, my silent companion, stood guard in my periphery. Ever since I'd abandoned my medication, he was inescapable, a shadow who haunted every corner of my vision. I roamed from place to place looking for Jendi, like a ghost searching for the living. The streets pulsed with life, each face a potential lead, a fleeting chance to find her. But hope was a disloyal thing, teasing me in the most unexpected moments.

In the dim glow of the train station, a homeless man muttered cryptic words that sent chills down my spine. "The past is a shadow," he rasped, his voice as weathered as the streets he slept on.

"It watches, it waits."

Khalid's presence weighed on me, a constant reminder of the past, as I handed the man a few dollars, his eyes unseeing but his words lingering.

At a bustling diner, I overheard a conversation that hinted at her whereabouts. My heart raced as I eavesdropped on two strangers discussing a woman with eyes like oceans who applied for a job there one night. But when I approached, their gazes grew wary, their whispers fading into hushed silence.

The city was a broken recording of lost dreams and broken promises. In the shadowy alleys of the red-light district, I glimpsed at a woman who had a striking resemblance to her. My heart skipped a beat, but as I drew closer, her eyes held only a small glow, nothing like Jendi's.

I had to make things right. I looked through all my old stuff and found some old paperwork and the envelope from the letter it said a motel but the name was ripped. So for the next three days I dialed every number I knew might lead me to Jendi. But each time, the cold, mechanical tone of a voicemail greeted me, amplifying my loneliness.

Through rain-slicked streets and darkened alleyways, Khalid and I prowled the city again. This time searching each neon motel sign became a beacon, promising answers yet revealing none. The only lead I had was she wrote to me from a motel in Afghanistan, Khalid taking the ride with me everywhere to find her. The silence between us grew heavy; Khalid had always been a silent presence, but ever since I'd stopped taking my meds, he never left. He had become inescapable, a brooding storm always at my side. Each glare, each grimace, was a reflection of the tempest inside me. But as days turned into nights, his constant company oddly became my anchor, grounding me in a city that seemed to have swallowed Jendi whole.

Forty motels, forty dead ends. But there was one more - a last haven in a sprawling list of possibilities. I pulled up to it, the neon flickering, hinting at faded grandeur and countless secrets. This was the 41st, the final hope.

CHAPTER NINE

The 'Round-Up Motel' stood starkly, like a relic from a bygone era: a hole in the wall, with expansive windows tinted by years of dirt and neglect, shielded by rusting bars on the outside of the glass. It didn't just look like a motel that time forgot; it felt like the underbelly of the city's history, a place where stories came to die. A chill ran down my spine as I touched the cold handle of my 9 millimeter handgun. Good thing I brought my pistol, this was the sketchy part of town in Topeka. The dark corners of this particular motel in the neighborhood were notorious, and the murky activity on display affirmed its reputation. There seemed to be more souls lurking outside than there were guests inside - hushed exchanges, secretive glances, and shadows moving with transactional purpose.

I pushed through the grimy door into the lobby, the smell of stale cigarettes assaulting me. It became immediately clear that asking the clerk for any useful information would be a waste of time. Her vacant eyes, struggling to remain focused, told a tale of substance abuse. Good thing Khalid stayed in the car; his angry face would have made me lose my patience with this druggy-working receptionist.

The sinking feeling in my gut grew heavier. "Excuse me," I called, trying to pierce through the thick fog surrounding the clerk.

She sluggishly lifted her head, eyes half-closed and slurred, "What?"

"I need to find Jennifer Dominguez. Is she here?" With significant effort, her hand wavered towards a tattered green logbook lying on the counter, the pages yellowed from age and use. She weakly motioned toward it, her head drooping back down.

With my heart pounding, I snatched up the book, scanning frantically through the recent entries. 'William'… 'Wheeler'… and then, like a lifeline, 'Jendi.'

"Yes!" I celebrated under my breath. A rush of adrenaline coursed through me. "She's here! She was here!" I whispered, momentarily forgetting the gravity of my circumstances. I almost wished Khalid was next to me so I could high-five him, but he remained outside, a silent guardian in the car.

Trying to make sense of the hastily scribbled room

number was like deciphering an ancient code. It was either the hand of someone utterly careless or someone under extreme duress.

Desperation laced my voice. "Ma'am, can you tell me what room number this is?"

She muttered something incoherent, barely louder than a breath. "14… something."

"What's this room number?" I asked, pointing to Jendi's scribbled entry.

"14… something," she mumbled, her voice trailing off.

"I need specifics. Now!" The edge in my voice surprised even me.

She took a labored breath. "…148."

"Thank you!" I said, though she seemed too out of it to even hear my gratitude. "Where's the key?"

But she was already gone, lost in whatever world she had retreated to. Pushing my annoyance aside, I spotted a worn-out drawer behind the counter, with room numbers on each slot. '148.' One slot was empty, the other held a key, waiting for me. I grabbed it, feeling the cold metal in its old school design, finally some forward movement in this rapidly unravelling puzzle. With the key securely in my grip, I headed out, the weight of what might await pressing heavily on my shoulders. The air was dense with a mix of cheap liquor, stale cigarette smoke, and the sharp scent of marijuana. Buzzing with the pulse of deep bass music and an undercurrent of danger. Everywhere I looked, shadows danced, an open bottle passed from hand to hand, and a group of guys seemed engrossed in filming some ghetto music video with their phones.

"148, where the hell is it?" My voice barely a whisper, drowned out by the surrounding chaos.

My gaze settled on a room number next to me that read 117. "Damn! Gotta go deeper into this mess," I thought. Looking at how the rooms were designed with outdoor windows covering most of the front of the rooms. My eyes quickly counted each door. My quick math showed the room was right by the group.

I felt the weight of the 9 millimeter nestled against my hip, reassuring and threatening at the same time. My fingers brushed over the handle, feeling the cold metal.

"You in this Khalid?" I glanced sideways, half-expecting him to be there.

His absence was like a void, making the scene around me even more unsettling. But I could sense him, almost like he was shadowing me, always close but just out of sight. The crowd's focus shifted subtly, a few eyes lingering on me too long, sizing me up.

The numbers didn't seem to follow a logical order. The closer I got to where the raucous gang held court, the more my heart pounded, thudding so loudly I was sure someone would hear it over the pounding bass of their music. Pushing forward with more urgency, I tried to blend in, pretending I had every right to be there.

I found myself unintentionally drawing nearer to their makeshift party.

Suddenly, a woman stepped into my path. High heels, too much makeup, and a dress that had seen better nights. She gave me a once-over, her expression calculating. "Looking for some company, honey?" she purred, reaching for my hand.

I sidestepped, quickening my pace, "I'm good."

Her smile vanished, replaced by eyes of anger and a mouth that matched, enough to draw a few glances. "What's the matter, cop? Can't handle the likes of me?"

CHAPTER TEN

Trying to ignore her, my focus locked onto the increasing room numbers. 147... almost there. As I neared 148, I ducked out of sight when I saw someone inside, avoiding the expansive window next to the door. Peeking through a gap in the curtains, that's when I saw her. Jendi. She was sitting on the edge of the bed, her posture tense. Another bigger silhouette moved in the bathroom, obscured by frosted glass and steam, but clearly in a hurry. Every second felt like an eternity, and I was aware that one wrong move could change everything. The uncertainty of what awaited inside that room made the night's chill feel even colder on my skin.

The raw urgency of the situation tightened its grip around me, making every sound amplified and every shadow a potential threat. The real challenge was about to begin. I could see Jendi was barely dressed in between the gaps in the steam on the window.

The din of the party faded to a distant hum as my eyes remained locked onto the window. The raw emotions tearing through me seemed to echo in the stark movements of Khalid's shadow. My heart raced, hammering against my ribs. Every silhouette, every movement in the room made me feel like a spectator to a dark play. I put my face to the window and watched as Jendi crawled towards some heavy set man now sitting on the edge of the motel bed. Khalid suddenly appeared in the room next to them, fuming with anger, breathing frantically as if he was possessed. I knew Khalid's presence in the room was impossible, I knew it, but the lines of reality blurred. The pressure built in my head a tempest of emotions crashing like waves. I felt as if I was teetering on the edge of sanity.

He shouldn't have been there, but his sudden appearance mirrored the storm of feelings churning within me. I could sense his anger—it was, after all, a reflection of mine.

As Jendi moved, it felt like Khalid's shadow was drawn to her; just as my own thoughts were consumed by her. The closer she got to the mysterious man, the more Khalid seemed to loom, as if trying to intervene.

"Damn it, Khalid, get away from her, there gonna see you" I whispered, my voice a hiss of desperation. The emotions he represented – my own pent-up fury and desperation – now seemed to be acting out in the room.

A distant shout from the partygoers snapped me back to reality. "Hey, what's up with you" They might not see Khalid, but they could see me, a voyeur peering into a world that wasn't mine. From the corner of my eye, I could see the party-goers pointing, their voices raised in curious concern.

"He's trippin'," someone laughed.

"Hey, man, you lost or something?"

Another voice called out, "Yo, who's that creep looking' in the window?"

I snapped back to them, heart in my throat. "It's my room," I mumbled, trying to dismiss their concern. The reality was that they were looking at me, but for a fleeting moment, my mind played tricks. I felt as if I needed to go in and get Khalid. If only they could see the storm of emotions he was grappling with inside this room they would be more worried about him than me.

My attention snapped back to the window. Khalid was closer to Jendi, his shadowed figure looming behind her like an embodiment of my jealousy. As she leaned into the unknown man straddling him on the bed, the tension in the room - and in me - seemed to ratchet up another notch. I felt Khalid's anger; it mirrored my own, boiling and raw.

"What's he doing?!" someone shouted, referencing my unwavering gaze into the room.

Ignoring the taunts, my focus returned to Jendi. The

more intimate she got with the man, the more it felt like a knife twisting in my gut. And every pang of jealousy, every ounce of anger, seemed to embolden Khalid's shadow in the room. The knife that felt like it was piercing my gut was now in his hands. It was as if he was trying to act on my behalf, to be the physical entity that could step in when I felt powerless.

My grip on the pistol tightened, a cold reminder of the power I had in my hand. But the real power was with Khalid, the rage-fueled figment of my imagination, that now seemed to be taking a life of its own inside that room. "Don't do anything stupid Khalid, please" I said, still looking on.

But the most unnerving part was the feeling that they might actually turn and see him - that for once, my inner demons would be visible to the world. It was a ridiculous thought, I knew. But in this heightened state of tension, the impossible felt all too real.

As I tried to make sense of the chaos unfolding in the room, a voice startled me from behind.

"Hey, what the fuck are you doing?" I turned sharply to find the dopey-eyed clerk, seemingly having awoken from her drug-induced stupor, glaring at me with unexpected clarity.

One of the party-goers, a wiry guy with tattoos snaking up his arm, squinted at me suspiciously. "Man's either a weirdo or a cop, cause he's been sneaking around like one."

A voice from the gathering crowd piped up, almost amused, "That's coqui's room, that's what the spanish boys call her, with her cute lil freaky ass!"

Confusion swamped me. "Coqui? Who the fuck is that?". Suddenly confusion hit me "Was I mistaken?" my mind raced wondering was this even Jendi in this room doing every man's worst nightmare, to see the love of his life do to another man.

I needed to focus and get a good look and no more distractions. With adrenaline surging through my veins and desperation coloring my actions, I raised the pistol, aiming it skyward. "I am a cop! Now back off!"

The effect was immediate. The clerk ran back to the office and the party-goers fell silent, some taking a step back, eyes darting between me, the gun, and the doorway of room 148. The heavy atmosphere grew even more charged, every moment stretched tight with anticipation and fear. I looked back into the room to confirm it was Jendi and all I could see was Khalid standing over her with the knife in his hand, and a woman riding a man who was smiling with pleasure.

"I have to intervene," I thought, my grip tightening on the pistol. A choice had to be made, and soon. The weight of my decisions pressed down, threatening to consume me entirely. The sudden blaze of blue and red lights cut through the darkness, catching me off guard. I could hear the roar of an approaching police car, every decibel echoing like a siren in my already overwhelmed mind. I could barely feel the gun in my hand, slick and wet from the sweat that had pooled there. Another glance inside the room, and my world shattered. It was Jendi, she was now face down doing things that showcased every man's darkest fears. The sting of betrayal, sharp and overwhelming, clouded my vision. I teetered on the brink, a rush of dizziness threatening to pull me under.

Everything else faded, I couldn't hear the police siren, I couldn't hear the chatter or the party's music anymore; the only sound piercing through was Khalid's frantic breathing and a mirror of my own broken heartbeats. For a moment, everything stood still, with Jendi in a scene that just punched me right in the gut.

My head spun, a mix of rage and disbelief. Why here? Why in this dump? Our past flashed by – the laughter, the fights, the love, the damn games, and the echoing silence of her absence. Suddenly, Khalid towered over the scene, knife in hand ready to strike, hovering ominously over Jendi and the man. My heart raced – I didn't want her hurt, not even now. But would Khalid listen?

The world snapped back as headlights blinded me. The cops were out, guns drawn.

"Drop your weapon!" one shouted.

I rushed, panic stricken, "They...they are in trouble inside there!"

The key felt heavy, ice-cold as I wrestled to fit it into the lock, every second extending into an eternity. Moans from the room clawed at my ears as I fumbled with the key to unlock it, the cops moving in towards me, every sound like a punch to the gut. A wave of nausea hit me, a toxic mix of jealousy, heartbreak, and anger. Busting open the door, the room's glaring light revealed the messy scene.

"Freeze!" The sharp command of a cop cut through the air.

But my focus was on Khalid, rising up like a dark specter behind Jendi, knife glinting menacingly.

"Khalid, don't!" My voice cracked, a plea edged with desperation.

Jendi's eyes locked onto mine, a cocktail of confusion, recognition, and terror. "Junior!"

I could see it all, in slow motion, Khalid's arm drawing back, the sharp blade aimed at her. Without a conscious thought, I turned the gun on Khalid, before pulling the trigger I remembered who he was, he was a part of me. Now he was attacking what I couldn't, he was doing what I was thinking. But I couldn't hurt Jendi. I loved her that much and I knew to really stop Khalid I had to stop myself. Thats when I put the gun in my mouth and shot Khalid in the head. The deafening blast echoed in the confined space. But Khalid wasn't real, and the bullet that was meant for him...

"Junior, NO!"

Jendi's scream sliced through the fog.

The room filled with the hectic noise of blaring sirens, frantic police radio chatter, and above all, the heart-wrenching sobs of Jendi. The fat Italian man she was sitting on starts sliding off the bed to cover the coke on the nightstand from the cops in the commotion. "Is everyone okay?" The cop, visibly shaken face full of sweat, asked with his gun in hand looking at Junior on the ground.

Suddenly Khalid disappeared. All that stood was a now blood soaked nightstand with the signs of a rushed transaction — wrinkled money, an open pack of cigarettes, and the glistening wrapper of a condom. A thin haze of cheap perfume and stale smoke lingered in the air, suffocating the atmosphere. The unkempt bed, with its twisted and stained sheets, bore silent witness to countless secret rendezvous. The gun was still smoking laying inches from Junior's head, his feet facing each other face down. The cop grabbed the door frame and yelled "Holy shit!"

Jendi looked up, eyes wide in surprise, tears pouring from her eyes. But the voice that rang out wasn't hers, it was the Italian man she was with— his voice was rough and dripping with a New Jersey accent, "Jesus Christ, he did it. The kid shot himself!" His last seconds of consciousness were the parking lot party goers camera phone lights. They were in the background and as he drifted away, they shined like star twinkles. Then everything began to fade, looking like the skyline in

Texas as junior and his dad cooked that majestic deer. That day was full of love, a great celebration between father and son, that day he got it right, that day he got "Junior's first kill".

II.
PEEPING TOM

CHAPTER ONE

Ever since my ex-girlfriend Sarah and I went through that heart-wrenching breakup, I felt an urge to distance myself from the quiet, countryside corner of Wyoming I grew up in. I'd heard tales of the dazzling new city of Netropolis. It was said to be the city of tomorrow, a dream for tech enthusiasts, with neon skylines that rose to the heavens and roads filled with levitating cars. I had dreamt of its holographic billboards displaying ads from the future, of its AI-driven cafes that knew your favorite drink before you even walked in, and of streets lined with robotic assistants performing feats no human could achieve. The stories hyped it up as a spot where the real vibed with the virtual, where every move dropped you into a next-level futuristic groove.

But as my bus pulled into the heart of Netropolis, I got a major reality check compared to those tales. True, the levitating cars were there, and the neon lights were as vibrant as described. But the people... they were all deep diving into their screenless virtual hologram phones, living all the time in their digital bubbles. No one looked up to admire the colorful spectacles or the wonders of this technopolis. At the hoverbus stops, in cafes, on the gleaming streets - everyone seemed to be living in a world inside their holographic screens. It felt like a city of zombies infected by a digital virus, rather than a futuristic metropolis boasting zero emissions, advanced AI integrations, and award-winning urban designs... at least that's how they advertised it in the congratulation's brochure.

I won a lottery pull the government helped hold once yearly countrywide for a chance to move to the new future city and it was a bust. My ex-girlfriend entered me into the contest before we split for her own selfish motivations and when I won the rare opportunity, I thought why not get a fresh start somewhere new? It's ironic because I happen to be the most antitech person there is. My TV still had a real screen on it, and I didn't even have a smartphone, I had what I liked to call a 'brick with benefits'. When I received the email about the application and acceptance, I was initially hesitant. However, the government was footing the bill for relocation alongside SocialChat, the new big Social media giant. Besides, what better place to start anew than a city created by an electric car guru and the world's most renowned social media titan and creator ever?"

The first day I moved to Netropolis, I thought it would be a rush, an immersion into a future I had only imagined.

Instead, all I found was a bunch of mindless bots talking about whatever was the new argument to have on their social feeds. It was disheartening. Everything seemed to be evolving technologically, but human connection in the city seemed to be unplugged. The first stop I made was the subsidized housing office like the instructions said to get my first free place in Netropolis. Filling out the registration form for assisted living, I was happy they gave me priority because I'm a veteran. I scribbled down my name "Adam DeMarco" – reflecting both my Italian and Puerto Rican heritage. Glancing over to the occupation field, I smirked and jotted down "struggling mixed martial artist."

The memory of past fights flashed before my eyes, each leaving its mark, especially the cauliflower-shaped trophies on my ears. My slicked-back black hair, a characteristic I proudly inherited from my father's side, glistened under the lobby lights. Standing tall my six foot one inch fighter's physique contrasted sharply with the hunched postures of those engrossed in their screens around me. Sure, I had come to Netropolis chasing big dreams, but this wasn't exactly the grand entrance I had imagined. With the city's staggering inflation, even those flaunting high-end jobs seemed to struggle. Exiting the registration center, I made my way to meet the "network creator" – Netropolis' slick name twist on landlord. As I traversed the buzzing streets, two thoughts weighed on me. How would a tech novice like me find my footing in this digital playground? And in a city so technologically advanced, why did everyone seem so disconnected?

CHAPTER TWO

When I won the raffle invitation to the city, it came with the perk of qualifying for government-subsidized housing and when I arrived the lease had more pages than a terms and conditions agreement for your favorite website. I almost didn't sign. A small overconfident landlord or "network creator" named Tom convinced me to live in one of his many buildings right next to each other. I walked in confused at the futuristic layout of his office as he extended his hand to greet me.

"Well, hello there Adam, I'm Tom," he spoke up confidently but as if he was expecting me. "I will be your first friend here I guess. Just pay attention okay?, So we're clear there is no rent here, just agree to the rules, sign, and you're good to go" his voice cracking as he finished his speech. Tom was the landlord for three 500 room apartment buildings that stood across from one another and he would lease them out to government housing contracts to make sure he got paid. Sometimes it felt like he had it under control and sometimes it felt like pure chaos.

After a brief introduction, Tom led me through the tunnel-like corridors of the apartment building to my door. The futuristic city of Netropolis had given birth to an odd mix of technology and urban decay, and Tom's building was no exception. The walls were adorned with holographic graffiti that seemed to dance with neon colors, creating a surreal atmosphere.

We finally arrived at the entrance of my new apartment. Tom waved his hand over a digital pad, and the door slid open with a faint hum. As he started the tour I realised the apartment was a stark contrast to the chaos outside. It was small but surprisingly clean, with minimalistic furniture that radiated a futuristic charm. Tom gestured toward the kitchen, which was equipped with sleek, stainless steel appliances. "This is your kitchen," he said, sounding almost proud. "You won't need to cook much; we have food delivery services that cater to every taste imaginable."

I nodded, trying to absorb the rapid changes in my life. The city, this apartment, and the technology were overwhelming. As I followed Tom into the living area, I couldn't help but notice a large, panoramic window that dominated one wall. It was like a massive screen, displaying ever-changing scenes of the city. Tom caught my fascination and grinned. "Ah, the EchoView. It's a masterpiece of augmented reality. For the right price you can change the view to whatever you like. If you're into sunsets, we can arrange that. If you prefer the night skyline, no problem. And if you're connected to Social Chat, your view will reflect the preferences of the people you follow." Tom turned to me and said, "All you have to do is stand in front of it, and the window recognizes you. No need for logging in or any passwords."

"EchoView," I interjected, my annoyance with technology creeping into my voice. I missed the simplicity of regular houses - wallpaper, traditional furniture, and windows that didn't require a digital manual. "How do I disable it" I said with a smirk, Tom rolled his eyes and continued with the tour walking down the hall still describing each fixture and wall. Curiosity piqued, I stood in front of the window, and it immediately flashed a cryptic message about not having an account, which seemed somewhat shady to me. The whole setup felt like an elaborate scheme to extract money from its users, but I had no intention of falling for it.

Tom chuckled, walking right up to my side as if he was used to residents like me. "You'll get the hang of it Adam. Netropolis has a way of growing on you. Now, let me show you the bedroom."

As we moved to the bedroom, Tom continued his enthusiastic tour, explaining the apartment's smart features and how to customize everything to my liking. After he left and the tour was over, I had a headache, I needed to take a walk and couldn't even figure out how to lock my door. I stood in the hallway waving my hands a few times in front of the pad on my door like a crazy fan as it flashed red, "I guess that means it's locked," I said, trying to make sense of the high-tech panel on my door. I looked around, half-expecting someone to pop out of their apartment and offer help. Down the hall, a man was walking towards me with his family, and something about his confident stride told me he knew his way around these doors.

"Hey there," I greeted him, eager to have a fellow tenant guide me through this new world. "I'm Adam, I just moved in here."
The man extended his hand with a welcoming grin. "Adam, nice to meet you. I'm Finn. I won the raffle to live here last year," he said, excitement still evident in his voice as he recalled his own journey to Netropolis. "These doors can be tricky at first. Just hold your hand in front of the panel until it recognizes you. No need for keys or cards."
As I watched in amazement, Finn demonstrated, placing my hand in the right place as the door obediently locked. My gratitude was noticeable by the relief on my face. "Thanks, Finn. I appreciate it. And this place... it's different, isn't it?"
Finn nodded, his eyes drifting to his wife and toddler

who were standing behind him. "It is, indeed. It's a world of its own, a safe world, a place where dreams, realities and fantasy blur. I moved here for a fresh start, for my family's sake." Emily, Finn's wife, walked away to open their own door. She possessed a classic, timeless beauty. Her graceful features and flowing chestnut hair gave her an elegant quality. With each step, she moved with the poise of a dancer, her bright eyes reflecting a gentle kindness that seemed to invite trust effortlessly. Both of us looked as she walked away. His words hinting at deeper stories, tales of triumph and struggle that lay hidden behind the glossy facade of Netropolis. As I said bye and watched Finn walk into his own apartment, small child in hand, all I could think was, "Wow, that guy has the dream – a beautiful wife and an adorable kid." I felt the hope that someday, I too would find that kind of peace and happiness. I placed my hand and head on my apartment door deep in thought, I turned and let my hand slide off as I began my walk. I took the time to look back at the building as I walked into the city.

I knew it wasn't the best place to live but it was free for me until I got on my feet. So, for the next year in the city, I made it... Myspace.

As I walked through the streets of the city one day after my boxing session on my way home from work, I could barely move through the crowds of people. It was like swimming against the current in a storm ready ocean. The city was getting overcrowded!

Everyone was nose down like a plane with no engine power getting ready to crash, it was like an analogy for the way their brains were crashing all looking at this device in their hands. But not me. I was old school and honestly not into this new digital wave. I rarely checked my cell phone and would gag at the ads trying to sell me new technology all throughout the city.

See, I've got this vintage phone a real relic, no frills. No apps, no games, no digital gimmicks. Just texts and calls, straight up. A brick in a world of glass. It ran like shit but the battery was amazing. I would forget to charge it for days and it wouldn't die. That phone had the David Goggin's of batteries, it never quit on me. I would often have to get it serviced at the local phone shop just to keep it up as it was the only store in town that would still touch the old style phone.

Today was one of those days.

I dropped it on my way to the subway and ever since then the normally green outdated dinosauric screen was black. I couldn't see a thing on that screen and I had a few calls to make about my upcoming fight.

I dodged the normal zombies coming in and off the train, eyes glued to their phone like the screen protectors people use to put on ever so carefully. See as I looked around I realized no one paid attention anymore. Everyone was either checking a new tweet or sending a pic of their surroundings. Shit I even saw a lady taking pictures while biting her food in different angles holding the camera for the perfect shot. Just to throw the food away right after posting it. A homeless man waiting for it so he can dig through the trash to calm his hunger pains. Myself and the cellphone repair shop owner, an old african man with long gray hair and a cane watching the scene unfold from the large phone repair shop store window. His name was Rapheal but as I got to know him over throughout the year I had been living in the city I called him Ralph, and he always had something to say. This time was no different as we watched on.

"This is the city's circle of life HA!" he shouted "it's Damn shame! and all for likes" I replied disgusted at how society has turned out these days. Ralph shrugs his shoulders as he walks behind the cell phone repair shop counter with his tools for fixing phones scattered around an old antique cash register. "What can you do?" The disappointment showed on his face as he spoke. "How long until I can pick it up?" I said, hopeful as I reached in my bag and handed him my broken cell phone as I always did. He took a few minutes to look at it and the condition it was currently in before he spoke with a sigh.

"Mr. Demarco, I have fixed this many times over, I'm afraid this phone might have run its course. It may be time to upgrade."
Just as he finished his sentence I snatched my phone off the counter and blurted out in anger "upgrade?

I hate all that new tech shit, No way! Come on old man, you can fix it. my voice went from mad to pleading."
With the assurance of the doctor giving a grim diagnostic he looked at me sternly as he spoke. "I'm afraid you might have no choice this time, Adam. I know a good place that will give you some good prices."

CHAPTER THREE

I threw my phone in my bag, stormed out of the store, and waited at the crosswalk for the green light. "The fuck did he mean upgrade?! I didn't want to upgrade!" I mumbled under my breath at the curb. People around me would see my anger if they weren't all in their little virtual worlds standing around me.

The light turned green and the sea of phone zombies came rushing towards me. I dodged all the non-attentive minds, digging deeper into other people's profiles or finishing the last level on their favorite games, not an excuse me spoken as they almost bump into you.

My head was spinning, I went and stopped at the one place where I knew real talk still existed. The barbershop! The only place where sports and current events were still talked about from the heart. None of this Google shit to see who was right! The place sat on the corner and

I could see it was packed through the glass window that showed all types of digital advertisements. It did not deter me from going in. Nowadays every place has been digitized in the past few years but this one still has its soul.

As soon as I walked in there was talk of Jordan, Kobe, Curry and Lebron being the Goats. And regular guys telling their outlandish stories while they waited for their favorite robot barber that can give a precision haircut based on a simple photo. I took my coat off and got comfortable. I sat in the only human barber's chair there. The place was packed with people and it was empty, already I could overhear this big fat Italian guy's story from the weekend.

 This is exactly what I needed, I leaned over to tune in to his conversation and so did the rest of the shop. "Okay, so I'm in the bathroom taking a pill so I can break this doll in half, right?" He sast up as he spoke, excited in his chair, "And yeah she was a fucking doll, couldn't have been no older than twenty-three or twenty-four years old tops," he now had the whole rooms attention as he continued.

"After the pill, I sit on the bed and she's crawling towards me on the floor in some silk lingerie shit and starts sucking my dick" he explained in detail the looks on everyone's face begging him to continue the story as a young teenage boy sweeping up started laughing as the man talked.

"I get on the bed and she rides me for the finishing move, then BOOM! Some whackadoo Soldier comes in and almost fucks my nut up". The room was now silent in suspense, the sweating man wiped his face with a cloth from his pocket before continuing.

"So he breaks in, gets to yelling pistol in hand with cops right outside...then BOW! Blows his own brains out!" everyone's face now turning as they react to the story. "What the fuck?" and "Damn!" all get yelled out from the barbershop crowd.

I sat as I got my haircut, remembering I saw this story on the news a few weeks earlier. Eager to hear the next part, I responded "That was you! That's crazy as hell! I saw it on the news. What did you do? Then what happened after? What did you do?" I asked, wanting all the answers at once and was surprised I was seeing the guy from a news story that shocked and saddened me.

"Hey take it easy!" the Italian man said in about the most New York accent you can have. "I said he almost fucked my nut up!"

The man then moved his hips in a sex motion as if to insinuate he kept having sex. The room broke out into laughter, but inside I was feeling weird and sad about the soldier.

"What do you want me to do? She was a whore, a prostitute, I heard she did the soldier bad, though.

It fucked him up her being a prostitute while he was deployed or some shit." The man was wiping his forehead and mouth with the cloth, sweating as if he had eaten a ghost pepper.

"I bet it was," a young veteran-looking guy spoke out as the Italian man continued.

"Relax G.I Joe" he joked before continuing . "I just so happened to be paying for a pussy, a girl that young, she was addicted to attention and dick like all of them nowadays. Jendi was her real name, apparently, the news said they called him Junior. I called her by her street name 'Coqui' or 'Starlight'."

The veteran now super interested asked puzzled "Coqui, what the fuck is that?"

The Italian man now the expert and center of the shop talk responded "Like the little frog in Puerto Rico, a coqui. They called her that 'cause she was small and loud," he again moved his hips to simulate sex.

"No chance you kept fucking," another man chimed in to the story as I paid for my now finished haircut. The Italian man stood up to go next in the barber chair and blurted out, "You kidding me I'm the Italian stallion."

We all laughed at how crazy it was, forgetting about our own problems. I guess real-life conversations had a way of doing that. Breaking my phone was already showing me that all the phone ever did was add to the distance and issues of society it was meant to fix. I walked out of the shop thinking about that Soldier. That story was crazy. Word from my former platoon is that guy and I were in the war at the same time. Different missions, same chaos. Fuck Jendi or Coqui whatever her name was.

"What a Hoe!" I said out loud, waving to the rest of the barbershop goodbye, grabbing my coat and pushing the door. My reality now kicked back in as I headed to the new cell phone store to replace my old broken phone.

CHAPTER FOUR

I made it to the store that was attached to the mini mall up the street from my apartment. The store workers all dressed alike and waved as I entered. I looked around the display for something I could understand, but there was nothing, how disappointing. All they had was the hologram this and the next generation that. I wanted the simple stuff. I grabbed the cheapest one they had and even that one was super futuristic to me. The store worker fired it up and the brightness was like a cool fire lighting up my face. It took my eyes a minute to adjust as the employee spoke up trying to help. "If you give me your old phone, I can transfer all your data over," he said with his hand out.

I pulled the old phone out of my pocket and placed it in his hand. Surprised at the age of the phone he grabbed it and said "Heavy! Man, this is a first gen, I am surprised it worked at all. Might be worth some money.

But I can't transfer data off this. You will have to input the numbers one by one, sir, sorry."

As I walked out with my super sophisticated, Netropolis citywide Netwave-connected, super smartphone, or whatever that means. I mumbled every curse I knew… "stupid mother fucker all this for a new useless piece of shit."

I pushed the button and fired the screen like hologram up. It was dark out now so the brightness hurt my eyes, like exiting a long dark tunnel and entering into the light from afar. It was blinding. I needed to add my trainer's number as soon as possible and I tried to remember the digits as I walked up the sidewalk towards my apartment. As I typed the last numbers in I felt the smallest softest body come head-on with me almost knocking my new phone to the ground. I looked up to see the most beautiful woman I ever laid eyes on. She had an arresting presence, embodying a blend of her African and Asian heritage. Her skin was a warm mocha, seamlessly blending her dual lineage. High cheekbones hinted at her Asian ancestry, while full, expressive lips which showcased her African roots. Her almond-shaped eyes, the color of dark chocolate, were framed by long, curled lashes that cast playful shadows over her delicate nose bridge.

She dressed in a fashion that immediately evoked images of a futuristic Comic-Con, taking the classic schoolgirl outfit and adding a touch of tomorrow.

The pleated skirt she wore wasn't made of any recognizable fabric but shimmered with holographic colors, reflecting light in a spectrum of rainbow hues with every movement. The blouse, a crisp white, was contrasted with metallic cuffs and a matching collar, flashing LED trims that seemed to be subtly pulsed to the rhythm of her heartbeat.

Around her waist, a utility belt featured an array of tiny gadgets, each looking like it belonged in the next century. Her stockings were translucent but displayed moving tattoos, animated patterns that slithered around her legs, spread around was code running from her thighs to her silver-clad high heel shoes. Those heels, one broken, besides adding inches to her height, hummed softly, suggesting they were more than just footwear.

Her curvy silhouette, emphasized by the tight-fitting, high-tech corset, added a touch of sensuality to the otherwise playful outfit. Her raven-black hair, streaked with shades of electric blue, cascaded down her back in waves, occasionally styled into intricate braids that seemed to incorporate fiber-optic threads, creating a soft glow around her face.

She was undeniably beautiful, not just in physical appearance but in the confidence with which she carried her unique style. It was evident she was a bridge between two worlds: one rooted in tradition and another reaching eagerly into the future.

Her soft, broken voice spoke up, "You better put a case on that?" I juggled my phone so as to not drop it when we collided. That's when I looked closer into her eyes to see the most innocent little angel still with mascara built up from earlier tears looking up at me.

"I'm sorry, excuse me" she said, her voice broken. "Are you okay? A bad break up?"

I tried to reply with confidence but was still taking in her beauty. She shook her head yes, looking down at her one broken heel and what looked like some tears on her LED-lit skirt.

"I'm Jewel", she said.

"Adam", I replied.

Jewel's face frowned, recalling recent memories. "Yeah, he was an asshole."

I was concerned by her sadness, so I responded gently, "I'm sorry, beautiful."

Suddenly, her eyes focused on something beside my face.

"What's that on your ears? Are you a fighter?" With a nod, I confirmed, "Well, yes. I'm actually a professional fighter." Her face lit up with mischief.

"Wanna kick his ass for me?"

Our shared laughter echoed in the empty street, the city lights playing off her face, revealing her true beauty beneath the remnants of tear-smudged makeup. Jewel, clearly intrigued, asked, "Can I have your number?" I didn't hesitate.

"Of course, it's 555-985-0786."

After a brief pause, Jewel inquired, "And do you have social chat?"

I was confused, "What's that?" But seeing her smirk, I quickly added, "I mean, I know what it is. I just... Well, I just got this phone, and I haven't set it up yet."

Jewel giggled, "Okay, okay. Set it up, and I'll be your first friend, Mr. Fighter!" as she held her hand out, "And where's your QR code with your info?".

The look on my face let her know I was as lost as a small boy on his first day of highschool. "I have a piece of paper?" I said with a smile. She wrote a quick note and handed me the folded paper playfully imitating a fighting stance, complete with a loud karate yell. I shook my head with a chuckle. "That site is just designed to melt your brain cells, you know?"

She made a dismissive gesture, "Some people have too many anyway!"

With that, she demonstrated a mock karate chop and began to retreat, her smile fading into the distance. She approached her building's entrance across from mine, and just before disappearing inside, she turned and yelled, "Text me on social chat!" She made a heart shape with her hands over her face. I have to admit I was taken by surprise, juggling my new phone, and trying to replicate her gesture. Then I was interrupted by her shout, "And get a case for that phone!" The door muffled her final words as it closed behind her.

Standing by the elevator on my way to my apartment on the 44th floor.

CHAPTER FIVE

I pulled the note she gave me from my pocket. It read, 'dreamy4422.' I grinned, replaying our interaction in my mind. I jumped onto my bed, eagerly launching the SocialChat app. After a series of awkward selfies from various angles for my face scan picture and wrangling with the app settings, a prompt appeared on the screen:

"Would you like SocialChat to control or assist in your apartment experience?"
Beneath the question, a brief description read, "This apartment is equipped with EchoView smart glass technology that allows integration with your SocialChat for a seamless living experience." Not entirely sure of what that entailed, I hesitated for a moment. I hadn't heard of this feature from Tom before. Uncertain and erring on the side of caution, I swiped "No," but the stupid

thing wouldn't register until I swiped sometimes. Then I resumed my search for her Dream4422... Dream4422 I saw her profile and pressed her name to be friends and follow her. She was so beautiful, and her profile picture was mesmerizing!

Distracted by the insistent meow, I turned to see Link, my moody cat. "Hey, Link!! You ready for some num nums?" Normally, that phrase would have her racing over to eat, but not now. Her expression was unmistakably human-like in her annoyance. It was well past her feeding time. In her displeasure, she jumped and made quick work of my curtains, pulling them down and shredding them as she stretched.

"Link! Damn it!" I yelled, torn between frustration and the desire to return to my virtual exploration. Upon returning my focus to the real world, I was drawn to the expansive window of my apartment, which presented an unobstructed view of the neighboring building. There she was! Jewel! She was vividly visible, moving in her space. I had never noticed I lived across from her before but when Link pulled the curtains down, I had a clear view directly across. Her silhouette was occasionally obscured by digital projections that flashed against the glass pane. Advertisements for products and services I didn't recognize played out in futuristic neon animations. There was an ad for a hoverboard, another for some virtual escape vacation, and yet another for a drink that claimed to boost cognitive abilities. This new age technology always left me feeling a step behind, and I couldn't decipher if these ads were generated from my window, from hers, or if it was just the way these smart apartments were designed.

Yet, amid this cascade of colors and visuals, it was Jewel who held my attention. The sporadic interference from these holographic displays, while distracting, only made the glimpses of her all the more intriguing.

I stood there watching as she moved gracefully, as if she were in a ballroom, perhaps dancing to a tune playing in her apartment. As she shifted, I caught sight of her unbuckling her bra beneath her shirt, her silhouette highlighted by the neon advertisements that occasionally played on her window. The perfect shape of her breasts showed through the shirt with her nipples hard as college arithmetic. These ads, integrated into the futuristic design of the apartments, projected tailored content for the tenant, but could also be a source of income if the tenant allowed them to display in their window. For a moment, the city outside disappeared, replaced by a holographic advertisement for a new brand of shoes, before it faded, bringing back the view of Jewel's room.

My cat's "meow!" snapped me out of it, her food bowl now runneth over as I started drooling seeing her bedroom from across my kitchen. The bedroom light went out and she left the room to explore her house in

a t-shirt and panties out of my line of sight.
Shaking my head, I turned away from the window, feeling an odd mix of guilt and intrigue. I needed a distraction. Something to focus my attention on. The recent events had spurred an idea, a need for change, the first page of my fresh start.

CHAPTER SIX

I walked over to my living room console for the first time and powered it up. Maybe it was time to give my space, whether digital or physical, a much-needed makeover. After all, if Jewel ever happened to look out and glance my way, I wanted her to see something worth her while. These smart apartments made it as simple as a click, it almost felt unreal. But I still spent hours deciding on the layout. The walls needed a fresh coat, something that resonated with who I was. After cycling through dozens of color palettes, I settled on a deep blue for the backdrop, contrasting it with a metallic silver for the trims.

Next, I focused on furnishing. A classic leather sofa, a vintage rug with intricate patterns, and some modern art pieces to hang on the walls. Each choice felt personal, a reflection of my character and my journey. The lighting took a bit more time. Did I want the soft ambient glow of a sunset, or the bright optimism of a sunny day? Maybe the calm of twilight? Decisions, decisions. I added some music to the background, setting the mood just right – a mix of old-school rock and a touch of jazz. As I arranged and rearranged elements, I thought of the visitors I'd have. I wanted them to walk in and feel at home, to understand a bit more about who Adam really was.

Once I was satisfied, I stepped back, admiring my handiwork. My space was now a beautiful blend of nostalgia and modernity, ready to be explored and experienced by those who'd drop by.

 I took a break to get a glass of water. That's when I saw her light was on.

What was she doing? Was she… She was standing topless in front of the window, looking down as if she was checking the traffic passing by below. Her breasts looked as perfect as white summer clouds against a blue background. "Whoa!" For a second, I lost my breath and spilled my water.

She looked up as if she heard me. We locked eyes and her face lit up like a diamond tester on a 3 quarter carat rock in the Jewelery store.

It felt like 30 minutes we stood looking at each other, her nude me completely aroused. She looked down as if she had gotten shy or she was checking the traffic again. An advertisement flashed, and when it disappeared, she was turned around bending over at just the perfect angle where I could see the imprint of her pussy against her panties. I could have fainted! All this for me?

"Man, she was hot!"

I grabbed myself and watched her on the bed, bent over moving back and forth. She would look back at me to see if I was still tuning in, then look up in the sky. She stood up, turned off the light and walked out of the room. I felt like I needed a cigarette.

 The next couple of days went exactly the same. Around 7 PM, I would stand watching her put on a live show, sometimes for minutes, other times for an hour, always looking down at the traffic, then performing for me. I started to prepare for the encounter: a bottle of lotion, and paper napkins, a chair with a cushion in my kitchen. I would look forward to this encounter all day, for a week then two. I sent a few fly messages on social chat, they all remained undelivered as if she gave me the wrong number.

I waited downstairs for the next couple of days and hung around the lobby hoping to run into her and I never did. But everyday, she would be there, sometimes naked, sometimes in lingerie. Performing for me. Teasing me.

I waited all day in my kitchen this time to see her. I purchased a wooden stick and got a sign to write a message for her. I couldn't think of the right things to say.

I'm horny..no... *I like you*..no...*I love you*.. None of these were the romantic words of Shakespeare I wanted to use to express my innermost feelings. I settled on just drawing a heart on the sign. I started holding it up when she would pose sexy or walk around in that tight white shirt and panties. I wanted to communicate with her so badly that I started holding it up when she was doing regular things or nothing at all, anything to let her know I liked her or to get her attention for a second. But when she would dress sexy and naked and pose, I would press that sign up against the window and let it stay there.

CHAPTER SEVEN

One day I got a message from Tom about an apartment upgrade. Tom the owner or digital creator like they say in Netropolis made me sync my apartment to the network. This is something they would force all the residents to do. Said it was a part of the terms and conditions and we had no choice but to comply or move out. I hated these upgrades because I never saw any difference plus I wouldn't be available to see Jewel when she was in her room in the evening if it took too long.

But today's upgrade was something else. When it was done in my kitchen, facing out to the other apartments, they'd fixed this odd button shaped like a heart.

"What's this, a 'like' button for my cooking?" I joked to myself. Beside it, a sleek keyboard appeared, with a note saying, "Interact with your neighbors!" I gave it a look over and saw a place to put my debt chip. To be honest, it all felt a bit out of my league. Back in Wyoming, my tech interactions were limited to changing TV channels. But here? It seemed I could send messages across windows. Why would anyone want that when you could just holler or wave? The future is strange. Then I got an idea, "This is how I can reach her".

With the apartments updated to allow window messages. I learned how to pay to write to her window directly. She would be performing as she always did and I would be typing how beautiful she is. Each time I pressed send I watched money drain from my account. I must have written thirty messages one day but they all got lost in a sea of other comments flooding in on the lower side of her window through advertisements. "That was a bust" I said half of my body facing the window as I made myself a sandwich on the counter.

"But it was worth it" I said, my voice muffled as I stuffed the sandwich in my mouth looking at Link on my counter.

From the corner of my eye, an ad flashed across Jewel's window. A grungy, stylized figure with a smirk emerged, dark shades masking his eyes. His name, "8 Ball," was splashed in neon green beside an array of colorful pills and powders. The caption read: "Instant Delivery. No Questions Asked." I frowned, leaning closer to my window. "That can't be legal to advertise on your window," I muttered finishing the last of my sandwich. Jewel's room became bathed in a radiant blue light, a clear sign that she was about to enter the room. I dusted my hands off, unzipped my pants and sat in the chair I had prepared for seeing her. As the lights intensified, so did her energy. With a drink in one hand, she swayed to the beats pulsating from her room, seemingly lost in the thrill of the moment. The more she drank, the more her movements became erratic, wild. She began to undress, dancing more provocatively. The room was bathed in a mix of colorful lights, almost like she was in some virtual club. Jewel's actions became even more erratic. She started to simulate sex on her bed and the comments went crazy under her window and I couldn't see my own. The more people wrote meant more payments and the wilder she went. Digital confetti started pouring from the top of her window. The lights in her room intensified, bathing her in a deep crimson color, with digital symbols I couldn't quite comprehend floating around her. However, spread throughout were a few digital "flags" or "reports" from the apartment building. No doubt this was breaking some kind of rule.

The weird advertisement for the "8 Ball," drug dealing guy appeared again blocking the whole window and showing "Get yours now. No wait. No hassle." I narrowed my eyes, trying to make sense of it. Then I yelled "Get this shit out the way", moving in my chair as if I could see around it. Suddenly, a massive digital red exclamation mark appeared in the center of her room window, blocking my view of her completely. The words "Account Suspended" blinked harshly, followed by a countdown timer indicating she'd been banned for 30 days. The vibrant lights dimmed, and her room plunged into darkness.

All that was left was a quiet silhouette. I could see her sitting on the edge of her bed, head hanging low. The previous energy was replaced with a somber stillness. I still pressed my apartment's updated digital heart button. I could send Jewel or anyone living in the buildings a heart for a small fee. It said denied on my window so I grabbed the slate I had originally drawn with the heart on when I first saw her and pressed my hand against my window, wishing there was some way I could reach out to her.

CHAPTER EIGHT

From then on she stopped showing up replaced by a timer on her apartment window I didn't fully understand. I would wait and wait and wait pressing the heart against the window when I thought I saw a light come on or a shadow pass by.

45 days went by and I began to get worried about her. Her ban timer was gone but all I would see was a light on from time to time and no glimpse of her. I would still sit and wait from time to time hoping that she would return a message or perform for me again.

One night after cooking dinner I was sitting backwards, my back leaning against the window facing my fridge. Link walks in and jumps on the counter pressing her body across my lap.

"You hungry girl?" her face lit up as I spoke like I guessed correctly.

I slid off the counter, heading to the smart-fridge for Link's food, when an odd light caught my eye, reflecting off the steel surface. Turning around quickly, I caught a glimpse of the light in her room dimming. Was she finally home?

This was the first sign of activity in 45 days. I pretended to do other stuff, often checking the kitchen window for signs of life. When her bedroom door finally did open I saw Tom pushing her into the room. She immediately started dancing and removing her clothes. This time it felt forced. Her actions seemed off. While she danced and undressed as usual, her movements were stiff, and awkward. And when she pressed herself against the window, I could see it in her eyes: distress. It wasn't the confident, sexy gaze I'd grown accustomed to, but a plea. She took her shirt all the way off and stood there naked now her arms spread out chest pressed up against the glass window I always watched her through. After several advertisements passed through the glass, I looked closer at her. She looked drugged. Acting instinctively, I pressed my new heart-shaped "like" button and placed my other hand against the window. Our eyes met across the digital divide.

In a soft, muted voice. She lipped two words to me that confirmed what I was thinking already... with her breasts still pressed against the glass she mouthed, "Help me!."

My brain raced, trying to decipher the windows and her possible room number to help her. I quickly calculated:

if my digital domicile was labeled 4524, and she is one building over she must be 4422. A memory flashed – the night we'd first connected when she gave me the folded paper with Dreamy4422.

The realization that she gave me her room number the first night when I asked for her social chat hit me like Ray Lewis across the middle.

I started running, tearing through the halls of my building like a bat out of hell, heading straight for Jewel's place. Every step I took was charged with urgency, my sneakers thumping against the shiny, metallic floors. The whole place, was lit up with this fake, bright light, but all I could see was Jewel's face in my head – scared, calling out for help.

Busting out of my apartment, I almost tripped over my own feet. I caught myself and kept moving, fast. The whole corridor felt off – flickers in the shadows, whispers sneaking out from behind doors. I wasn't the only one on edge; something was up, and it wasn't just me noticing.

The elevator, this fancy thing called 'The AeroLift', was crammed full of men with desperate faces trying to get a ride. No way was I waiting for that. Time was ticking away, she needed me now and I felt it slipping away. So, I hit the GlideStairs instead. These stairs are like something out of a sci-fi movie, all lit up and smooth. They were a way better option, floating me down quick, away from the crowded lift.

Hitting the courtyard, the cool night air hit me hard, a total flip from the stuffy building air. I was gasping for breath but couldn't slow down. This was a race, and I had no clue who I was up against.

Two guys, looking just as wired as I felt, were running from their building alongside me. When I went to run pass, the man pushed my chest boosting his own sprint. I immediately went competitive, on instinct I tripped the one who pushed me and sprinted around the other, sliding past a person calmly leaving the exit door to jewels building and slamming through the exit first. The door banged shut behind me, sealing those guys on the other side. Through the glass, they looked sweaty ticked off and desperate.

Their muffled screams of curse words blurred by the glass. Then I heard someone yell my name. "Adam!" It was Finn, my neighbor, the guy with the perfect family who had helped me lock my front door that day. He was pounding on jewels building exit door with those two guys who raced me here and more arriving, all yelling about someone needing help.

"Who needs help?", I shot back, but I couldn't stick around for answers.

I turned away and kept moving. Saving Jewel was all that mattered. The noise behind me was getting louder, like everyone was losing it. But I had to focus. I took the GlideStairs two at a time, their glow guiding me, my mind set on one thing – finding Jewel.

The 44th floor was like stepping into a different world – dead quiet, kinda eerie. It was nothing like the crazy scene downstairs. My heart was hammering as I raced down the hall, all my attention on door 22. But what I found there? It blew my mind.

Right at the door, things got real. Two guys were busting into Jewel's apartment. Fist clenched, I flew through her door behind them, ready to protect my girl, only to be met with confusion. This wasn't Jewel's apartment at all; it was some regular family's place. Not Jewel's, just a typical family trying to have dinner. Chaos erupted. The dad stood up, looking scared and mad all at once, shouting, "Get out!" His voice was desperate, but man, it was like yelling into a storm.

Then more guys started flooding into the apartment, like a wave, asking where Jewel was. And that's when it hit me. This whole scene? Everyone was here thinking they were saving Jewel. She wasn't even here. She was out there, somewhere, possibly in serious trouble, and we'd all been played by EchoView for our Social Chat.

It was a rough moment, realizing that. The unrestrained neighbor I thought I was connecting with? She wasn't real. She was just a face on a screen, a performance for everyone and no one. And I'd fallen for it, hard.

In the middle of this mess, with people yelling and this family freaking out, I felt this deep sense of loss. The Jewel I thought I knew, the one I'd fallen for, she was just an illusion. But that didn't make it any less real for me.

I knew then I had to find her, the real Jewel. I had to break through all the lies and the digital make-believe. Social Chat had been playing games with us, but now it was my turn to step up. I was going to find Jewel, the real person behind all this, and save her.

So, I pulled myself away from that crazy scene walking past more men running to what they think is Jewels apartment. My head was heavy, but my resolve? Stronger than ever. I remember I saw the ads for a meet and greet slide across her window she was having in a week. I knew this was how I was going to find Jewel, no matter what it took. This digital nightmare wasn't going to win. Someone had to save her from this.

Back in my apartment, I slumped against the window, my mind racing. The echo view – my digital window to Jewel's world – now felt like a blatant lie. For the first time I flicked through the background settings, each scene was more artificial than the last. Beaches, cityscapes, starlit skies – all just pixels, nothing real. I never switched it since Tom first set it up.

Hesitantly, I switched to the regular world view. The stark reality crushed me. My breathtaking view was nothing but a bleak concrete wall. Claustrophobia clawed at my chest, the walls of my apartment closing in on me. I felt trapped, not just in my apartment, but in the web of deceit spun by Social Chat.

Desperate to escape the suffocating reality, I flicked the view back to Jewel's place. That's when it caught my eye – the same ad that kept playing on her window. 'Creator Meet and Greet – See Jewel, and Nivia in person, and all the top creators of Netropolis.' It was all there, hiding in plain sight.

I couldn't believe how blind I'd been. The signs, the ads – they were clues to a larger, more sinister reality. It wasn't just about Jewel; it was bigger than her, bigger than all of us. But one thing was clear – Jewel needed help, and I was the only one who seemed to care.

I stared at the ad, my brain working overtime. If there was a meet and greet, maybe that was my chance. My chance to see the real Jewel, to help her out of whatever mess she was caught in.

Determined, I stood up, shaking off the feeling of confinement. I had a new mission now. I was going to that meet and greet. I was going to find Jewel. And this time, I was going to save her, not just from her digital prison, but from whatever was pulling the strings behind this beast controlling everyone.

And at the very least I was going to see if jewel was the real woman I met outside that day and now knew through my screen, or just a tool used by what seemed to be a giant monster disguised as a city.

The day of the meet and greet I felt nervous. It was like walking into a high-tech job fair on steroids. I forked over a hundred bucks for the entry – a small price for a chance to save Jewel. Inside, the place buzzed with activity. Drones scanned me for weapons as so-called Content creators of all kinds were showcasing their stuff. Each Creator had a booth, some were doing live shows, others were chatting with fans. It was a digital circus, and I was on a mission.

I looked around quickly to see some of the other creator's booths and it was a madhouse, some looked like churches others looked like sex dungeons complete with the latex suits. One station was a nasty brown color with what looked like a science project on a table, the creator looked lost and out of place, the smallest crowd waiting on edge for her next move, probably part of her act. These people disgust me arrogant talentless and entitled. But not jewel she was different we connected that day.

The biggest, most crowded booth was at the center. The closer I got, the thicker the crowd became, the noise rising to a fever pitch. Holograms and pictures of Jewel were everywhere. "Who was this girl?" I stopped to question myself as I took in the sites. Then I looked around and there, in the middle of it all, was Jewel and another girl named Nivia posing. She looked out of it, slouched in her chair, a forced smile on her face. Around her were guys, mostly leering men, waiting like vultures. My stomach twisted in disgust.

I asked someone where the line was to meet her. "Extra fee for that," they said. Didn't matter.

"I'll pay whatever," I said, my determination unwavering.

Finally, it was my turn. Jewel's eyes lit up when she saw me, a flicker of recognition. The event coordinator was setting up for the picture. Leaning in close, I whispered, "Come with me, Jewel. I'm here to save you."

She hesitated, then recognition dawned in her intoxicated eyes.

"You're the guy I bumped into once… I unfollowed you because you never post."

"I'm new to this," I shot back, feeling that undeniable spark between us.

Her voice dropped to a whisper. "Even if I wanted to leave, they'll find me." She nodded towards a tiny computer-like device clamped around her ankle.

Before I could say more, the coordinator was on me, saying time's up. Jewel managed a small smile and waved as I was escorted away. In that brief interaction, the reality of her captivity hit me like a freight train. I walked away, my mind racing with plans to free her, no matter the cost. I waited patiently in a crowd of stragglers as the convention drew to a close, my eyes never leaving Jewel. The energy in the hall slowly died down, replaced by a sense of tired resignation from the content creators as they packed up. They were herded like cattle onto a sleek, futuristic bus, each one looking more exhausted than the last. Jewel and the other creators boarded the hovering bus, its sleek contours cutting a sharp silhouette against the neon-lit skyline of Netropolis. Its engines hummed a low, futuristic melody, vibrating with hidden power. I lurked in the shadows, my senses heightened, as the vehicle levitated off the ground, its underbelly glowing with a soft, otherworldly light. I watched, my anxiety mounting, as it gently rose.

Frantically, I approached a nearby transport service, my voice edged with urgency.

"Follow that bus, and don't lose it," I instructed, my words clipped with desperation as i scanned my wrist wallet to pay. The pilot, sensing my urgency, nodded and quickly maneuvered his own sleek craft into the air.

Suddenly, my phone buzzed with a notification, snapping me back from my frantic thoughts. It read Jewels online, I clicked and it was a video of Jewel, appearing on my screen like a digital shadow. She was in her apartment, standing in front of a window overlooking the city. The exhaustion in her eyes was obvious, She hid them well behind her forced smile. She was dressed in skimpy clothes, her appearance blatantly manipulated to appeal to the masses, and way different from the posture I just saw. She seemed forced again, someone making her perform as she thanked people for attending the convention. Now that I seen the bracelet and know I could see the scene was a grotesque display of control and manipulation.

My grip tightened on the phone, anger boiling within me. This was no longer just a rescue; it was a mission to reclaim dignity and freedom.

As I exited the taxi ride, I spotted a service entrance on the side of the building and made a beeline for it. My heart pounded in my chest as I slipped inside, hoping to blend in with the night-shift workers. I kept my head down, avoiding direct eye contact with anyone, but I could feel the weight of the security cameras tracking my every move.

I ducked into a stairwell and began my ascent, the only sound my boots echoing on the metal steps. I was close now, so close I could almost feel the digital pulse of Jewel's apartment.

As I reached Jewel's floor, I heard footsteps approaching. Panic surged through me. I pressed myself against the wall, holding my breath as two security guards walked past, deep in conversation. I waited, counting the seconds, until their voices faded. That was too close, I thought to myself nervously.

The shimmering node, 4422, radiated with its unique 'dream' sticker. It was the same emblem I'd seen in advertisements all over Netropolis, touted as a must-have for all the popular Netizens.

Panic washed over me as I yelled, "Jewel!" and pushed through her door that looked digital but felt real.

I kept the handle turned walking in the door. It swung fast snapping closed behind me, the handle disappearing in it. When I turned around I was surprised to see the apartment was mostly empty. It was so strange to be in her place but it didn't feel like hers at all. The inner walls of her rooms were plastered with many digital images, each shimmering with its own soft lighting. I saw countless selfies of Jewel, each with exaggerated smiles and perfectly tuned filters that made her skin glow and her eyes unnaturally bright. Cats, probably viral ones from some meme or another were mid-leap, stuck in never ending animation over her countertops. Videos of beaches, mountain trails, and cities streamed by though they felt more like catalog pictures than genuine memories. Many were likely locations she'd never even visited.

In the midst of the overwhelming digital collage, one couldn't ignore the swarm of floating heart reactions and comments. A constant stream of affirmation and validation. I moved cautiously through the apartment, feeling the oppressive weight of the digital world she was trapped in. It was then that I stumbled upon the hidden room, where Jewel sat, her eyes wide with a mix of fear and hope.

Suddenly Tom's pixelated form materialized out of nowhere like a hologram in Jewels apartment.

"Adam, you're violating the Netropolis building Code of Conduct. This is her space."

Ignoring him, Amidst all the digital chaos, I bursted into the bedroom where I saw her most Jewel looked so out of place. Vulnerable and real in a room full of curated perfection. Tom emerged again in holographic form his avatar perfectly tailored as always.

After spotting her in the bedroom, I rushed to her side, pulling a digital robe from the ground to drape around her.

"Are you okay?"

"You came," she whispered.

"Yes," I replied, my voice steady despite the adrenaline still coursing through my veins. "And we're going to get you out of here."

Tom's voice crackled with interference,

"You think you're some kind of hero? This is her choice. Netizens here embrace freedom and show whatever side they wish."

Jewel's voice, weak and broken, cut in, "Not like this, Tom. This wasn't my choice." she turned into my chest and I felt warm inside as if i was holing a soft blanket fresh out of the dryer.

As I held Jewel close, a beep from my personal notifications to my new phone distracted me. Glancing back, I saw an alert message in my apartment windows viewing port. My mail icon was flashing urgently. A message from my training partner:

"Adam, careful! Many eyes on you!" It read. "How could he see me?" My face was puzzled at how he could see what I was doing.

It was then I realized we weren't alone. The countless

viewports of the Netropolis network were all focused on us, hungry for drama, thirsty for content.

Tom smirked, "Welcome to the main event, Adam. Every byte of this is being streamed, shared, and liked." I turned around to face Jewel's window and the moment my eyes pierced Jewel's digital glass, it felt like I'd dived headfirst into a turbulent sea of raw human emotion. Waves of desires, judgements, envy, and hunger crashed over me. The sensation was dizzying. As my vision focused I saw everything, thousands of rooms with different desperate faces in each one all looking at me now. Some guy jerking his dick, his face full of rage, yells for Jewel, others sitting watching the show. I felt all the attention and eyes on me at once. It was intoxicating, like a digital high. I could see why so many were addicted to this realm. The thrill of being watched, desired, and validated by an unending sea of faces was overwhelming. Rage and lust etched across their features, screaming Jewel's name and sending hearts.

As some of the viewers cheered a strange warmth spread across my body, an intoxicating blend of adrenaline and the rush of being the epicenter of so many eyes. It was the kind of attention that could easily draw you in, distort your reality, make you forget who you truly are. Seeking a lifeline, my gaze landed on my own digital space and the familiar heart sign I made from a paper and stick within it. That simple emblem grounded me, pulling me back from the edge. I turned back around to see the real Tom now holding Jewel, smiling. He was the orchestrator of this digital deception and must have snuck in when I was distracted. He was now clutching Jewel as if she were just another asset in his virtual empire. The boundaries between this digital world and reality seemed to be fading, but I was more resolved than ever to protect Jewel's humanity amidst this chaos. With a push on Tom's wrist Jewel's window slammed closed. A darkness took the apartment.

Tom, grinning maliciously, tightened his grip on Jewel.

"You're in over your head."

I pushed them apart and wrenched Jewel free from Tom, escorting her out of the digital prison she lived in. Before walking out I stopped and cut the ankle bracelet off her leg. A strong tan line remained from how long it was there. As i threw the bracelet at tom, she looked up at me with the most grateful eyes as if I had broken the chains holding her back. Her digital robe flickered as we left the apartment, her body almost fully exposed as I carried her wrapping her in my jacket her hugging me close, face full of relief. "Did you feel it?" she whispered. Her digital eyes glistened with gratitude.

"The weight of a million digital eyes?", I looked down at her angelic face and whispered, still processing and carrying her away.

"Yeah, I felt it."

Holding Jewel close, I felt a rush of emotions I had never

felt before. Her digital eyes seemed to hold galaxies within them. I tightened my grip, not wanting to let go. "Jewel," my voice trembled, filled with a vulnerability I hadn't known I possessed, "I... I want to live with you." I swallowed hard, watching her for any hint of a reaction. "What do you think?", I asked.

"Let's hear your point of view Jewel."

CHAPTER NINE

Adams' words echoed in my ears, mixing with the rapid beats of my heart. Living together? I have always been Jewel, a strong independent woman. To be totally real, the whole concept was a crazy mix of scary and, well, crazy. It was like stepping onto a runway in heels for the first time, thrilling because you're owning your space, but also kind of scary because, what if you trip? But hey, that's the essence of life, right? A blend of 'wow' and 'what the heck am I doing?' Plus Adam was great. Here was a man, real and tangible, offering a life away from the relentless pixels and notifications. A life in the true essence of the word. I met his hopeful eyes with mine and whispered, "With you, Adam? A life in high-definition? Let's do it."

The newfound freedom with Adam was intoxicating, far from the pixelated chains that had once bound me. I kept the bedroom curtains pulled down and closed at all times, I felt I needed my privacy from the world. I tried to not connect the new apartment we got to social chat but with the new apartments in Netropolis every place had to be on the net now, and a message would pop up. This is for integration with your SocialChat for a seamless living experience in your apartment. We had a different network creator or landlord but all the same show. I love my freedom now. When I moved in with Adam, I felt the connection and bond immediately. Our new apartment was an oasis, and I relished every moment, away from the prying eyes of the virtual world. The curtains, once a portal to scrutiny, now stood as guardians of our solitude. I didn't even think about Tom's place. Adam took me dancing downtown and to sing karaoke. All I could think of was how amazing he looked and how this moment should be remembered. With Adam, life was an orchestra of emotions, from whirlwind nights dancing beneath the city lights to harmonious days lounging by the ocean. His eyes held a genuine depth that contrasted starkly with the superficial glow of digital likes and follows. It wasn't about garnering attention, but about the quality of the connection. Yet, the blinking lights beneath the curtains remained, persistent, like an itch I knew I shouldn't scratch.

I went to bed that night smiling, lights under the curtain begging for my attention through the cracks in the curtains. I paid it no mind and turned hugging Adam.

Some days we went swimming in the ocean and laying in the sand. It felt like Adam and I were growing a great bond together, the loving eyes and one man's attention. He treated me amazing, I would often wish everyone knew how well he treated me and how sexy he was and that he was mine. I saw the notification lights flash under the curtain for months at night while I lay in bed paying it no attention.

But with Adam by my side, the allure of those beckoning lights faded. I was more immersed in the present, feeling the warmth of his touch and the genuineness of our bond. The digital realm had its pull, but with him, reality was so much sweeter. Even the nights I would hold him tight as he had nightmares from his PTSD he got from the war wiping his forehead with a wet washcloth.

I would be lying if I didn't say that some days I felt something was missing, and most days I missed my independence.

After weeks of brushing those thoughts to the side i started seeing how life with Adam was a stark contrast to the digital whirlwind I'd been swept up in. The city's neon glow, once a beacon of my virtual existence, now seemed distant, a mere flicker against the reality of our shared moments. Adam's presence grounded me, his touch a reminder of the tangible joys of life away from the screen.

Yet, as we walked hand in hand, the city lights shimmering in the distance, I couldn't help but feel a tug at my heartstrings. The digital realm, with its endless streams of adoration and validation, whispered to me, a siren song of what I had left behind.

As I had more nights with Adam, I learned they had their own rhythm, marked by his struggles with PTSD, remnants of a past marred by conflict. I would still hold him close, wiping his brow with a damp cloth, feeling the weight of his nightmares. In these moments, our connection deepened, transcending the physical to something more profound.

But in the quiet of the day, a sense of longing crept in. There were moments when Adam's laughter filled the air, his eyes alight with joy on our dates, and I would feel disconnected, my thoughts drifting away. I'd catch myself gazing at the city skyline, the window acting as a portal to my former life. It was more than just the lure of fame; it was the independence and identity I had carved out in that digital universe.

As Adam shared stories, his voice animated with excitement, a part of me yearned for the life I had left behind. The thrill of being in the spotlight, the rush of connecting with millions at the touch of a screen – these were things I missed. The window in our apartment, a silent observer to our lives, began to symbolize a gateway to that lost world. Each glance towards it was a reminder of the duality of my existence - the physical presence with Adam and the digital persona that still lingered within me.

Did I miss the worship, the constant attention and the validation from virtual strangers? Or was it the freedom to be whoever I wanted to be in the digital realm, unbound by the constraints of reality?

These thoughts haunted me, a quiet turmoil beneath the surface of our idyllic life. The window, once a mere part of our home, became a metaphor for the choice I faced the allure of the digital world, always just a login away, versus the genuine, however complex life I had with Adam. The struggle between these two worlds was a silent battle, fought in the depths of my soul, with each passing day.

CHAPTER TEN

One morning, a fog seemed to form around my consciousness that lasted all day. Even when Adam brought me joy, it felt like a hologram - shimmering, intangible. While he whipped up delicacies with his new culinary implants I taught him how to use one night, I just wasn't hungry. An unsettling stillness crept inside me. It felt like the calm was getting to me.

The bedroom's digital curtain displayed vibrant nightscapes, but I often found my attention diverted to a pulsating red glow slipping through its pixels. The morning of augmented run the new fitness feature this apartment added, Adam's voice broke my trance.

"Push through, Jewel! It may be a virtual run but the fatigue is real don't let it slow us down!

He was yelling for me to keep up doing his version of a motivational movie role but his every word was annoying me. I played it off as if it was helpful but that only encouraged him to get louder.

His augmented shouts, designed to motivate, Just got on my nerves. "Enough!" I snapped, halting.

I walked to the back and showered. I heard Adam walking up but I didn't want to be bothered so I closed the bathroom door.

After showering and cooling down. I immersed myself in the bathroom's mood-enhancing mist, wanting solitude.

But the truth? I was fracturing, like a glitching screen. falling apart. One night as Adam slept I layed next to him, my eyes wide open. Every once in a while seeing hours fall off the clock 1AM... 2AM... 3AM....

The neon glow of the city merged with that insistent red blinking from the corner of the room. Then it would go away. I went to pee and came back to bed even more restless.

There was that blinking red light again. I saw it out of the corner of my eye and now my head and eyes lie sideways fixated on it. With every blink my curiosity grew. It was so familiar but still so mysterious. The bright red lights flickered underneath the blinds and grew more frenzied, pulling me in like a moth to flame. Soon I found myself standing right in front of the window, both of my hands ready to pull the curtain up and see what or who is causing this red light to flicker, but I knew what was causing this red flickering light, "Or did I?"

I stood before the curtain, trembling. Deep down, I knew the source of this glow. But I needed to see, to confirm. This feeling was all too familiar, "I am important, my life is the most important, people see me, people like me. I hope they like me!"

One...two... three...

Jewel deleted the curtain and when she did, light poured into the room waking up Adam. When she could focus it revealed a sea of windows just like her apartment before. Everyone tuning to see her new apartment now mostly men drooling, licking their windows desperately. There it was again. Countless eyes started pouring in filling up the window. Digital and organic. Faces twisted in lust and obsession. Screens blazed with "Welcome Back" and leering emojis. All wanting her attention, waiting, watching. The underbelly of the digital age. One proud face stood out amongst them, smiling, looking, waiting, your first friend...

Peeping Tom.

III.
MAILMAN MICHAEL

CHAPTER ONE

As dawn breaks on a late August morning in California, the sun inches its way up over the horizon, and its warm light fills the sky turning it a cozy shade of gold. Palm trees dance to the rhythm of a soft breeze that carries the fresh smell of the ocean. The peacefulness of the moment is confirmed by the nostalgic beats of Will Smith's "Summertime," pouring out from a red drop-top convertible. The car cruises past a barely noticeable ordinary mail truck parked on the side of the road.

The atmosphere is thick with humidity, a countdown to the scorching heat that promises to define the day. But, within the sliding doors of that seemingly ordinary mail truck sits a man to whom this perfect setting is little more than a backdrop, a man whose secrets are as dark as the approaching noonday sun is bright.

In the cab of that mail truck in full postal uniform, not a button out of place is Michael. He takes a moment before walking out on his daily route. His eyes lock onto a laminated newspaper article taped to his windshield, a constant reminder of his past triumphs. The headline proudly proclaims, "Stockton, California's Mailman of the Year," accompanied by a photograph of Michael brandishing a bonus check for a thousand dollars, his reward from a grateful city.

"I still got it," Michael speaks out loud to himself, tapping the article lightly with his fingertips as if to draw strength from it.

Right next to the article is something less celebratory: a crumpled Netropolis sweepstakes entry ticket with the disheartening stamp of 'Not a Winner.' Netropolis, the invitation-only gleaming city of tomorrow reflected on it. It is a place that Michael had heard about, and like everyone aspired to live in the so-called tech paradise, an elusive dream when placed side by side against his current reality. For a moment, the sting of that failed lottery crosses his face, but it's quickly replaced by a smirk when he looks back at his mailman of the year achievement. "Let's do this" he says tapping the newspaper again, Michael steps away and catches his reflection in the rearview mirror of his mail truck. His black hair is very different from the sandy or brown locks so often seen on those considered 'conventionally' handsome. Micheal saw in his reflection that his face had grown more defined over the years. He's put on muscle, trading a leaner build for one that implies strength, both physical and emotional.

Though the man in the mirror shares the same smile as the guy in the old newspaper article, they are fundamentally different. One existed in a world of neatly sorted letters and community appreciation, and the other lived in a realm of darker urges and moral complexities.

As he adjusts his aviator sunglasses and takes one last glance at his Mailman of the Year article, it's clear that while the core of him might be the same, the layers have shifted, and evolved. What remains consistent is a sense of purpose, though its direction has veered into a path less straightforward, filled with shadows and questions.

Energized, Michael swings open the truck door and grabs his mailbag. As his mailman-issued boots touch the ground, he feels the immediate warmth of the sun radiating against his skin, causing sweat to start beading on his forehead. The streets are clear, and empty, with very few noises, only the sound of an occasional car cruising by. Trees dot the sidewalk, their leaves creating uneven, inkblot-shaped shadows on the ground. These dark patches offer brief escapes from the relentless sun, as if nature conspires to keep Michael's true self in the shade. Michael locks up his truck and starts his route. On the surface, it's just another day of delivering mail, nothing out of the ordinary. But hidden behind this mask of normalcy is a darker, more sinister agenda that nobody suspects. The houses in the neighbourhood are quiet and still, their windows closed against the heat. The only sign of life is the occasional chirping of a bird or the distant sound of a dog barking. As Michael walks by perfectly manicured lawns and gardens, with sprinklers turning on here and there to quench the thirsty grass.

 The heat of the morning presses down on Michael's shoulders, and he can't help but feel a sense of restlessness. After his first block, he already longs for the coolness of air conditioning, a cold drink to quench his thirst, and a distraction from the monotony of his daily routine. As he goes about his deliveries, his eyes naturally scan the surroundings, always alert for what catches his attention most, the beautiful women. Specifically, the girl-next-door types with blonde hair and blue eyes were his favorite to look at. There's even a certain bounce in his step, the casual stride of a single guy enjoying his day. He waves to neighbors who are busy fussing over their meticulously designed lawns and useless garden figurines. To anyone watching, Michael seems like just another friendly face in the community, effortlessly blending into the fabric of everyday life. He finishes the neighborhood and gets back In his truck to the relief of its struggling AC. The first neighborhood on his route is now complete.

"Thank God for AC" Micheal said to his water bottle as he guzzled the now warm water. Michael starts the engine and drives his mail truck through the suburban streets, lost in thought. Memories of his childhood flood his mind, and he struggles to keep them at bay. He knows that dwelling on the past will only lead to trouble, but sometimes the memories are too strong to ignore.

CHAPTER TWO

As Micheal's route takes him into the fancier more affluent neighborhoods, his eyes are captivated by the gorgeousness of the elegant homes that line the streets. But even that's a distraction, what truly commands his attention are the gorgeous women who grace the doorsteps of these residences. With their flowing hair and impeccable figures, they awaken something within him, an urge that's both magnetic and indefinable. To the casual observer, he's merely appreciating the finer things the neighborhood has to offer, but under the surface, a far more complex and unsettling emotion simmers. He's very aware that he knows more than just addresses and zip codes. With a nearly photographic memory, he can place each woman on his route, recalling not just where she lives, but what she looks like, down to the most minute details. It's a catalog of faces and homes that he has committed to memory, a roster that he keeps in his mind like a werewolf in case he transforms uncontrollably and needs to feed his darker, insidious cravings. For Michael, the allure of these women goes beyond mere attraction or even longing. It's not a case of a single man seeing a possibility, should the right opportunity arise to say hello and possibly date. No, for him, it's a compulsion, a necessity. He feels as if he needs these women. From the outside, it might look like simple infatuation, a typical response to beauty. Yet, within the depths of Michael's psyche, this need is much more troubling, an unsettling yearning that he can't quite put into words but feels compelled to act upon. Ever since he was young and what he saw before his mom went away.

He tries to push these thoughts from his mind, wiping his sweat with a paper towel in his truck while driving, but they linger like a persistent itch. He knows that he shouldn't be thinking these things, that he should be focusing on his job, but the urge is too strong to ignore. Navigating his mail truck down the familiar suburban road, Michael found his usual parking spot taken by a blue minivan. Slightly annoyed but still on the lookout, he was forced to park in front of a beige house with an immaculate lawn.

It was then that he saw her for the first time, a woman whose beauty struck him like a physical blow standing in front of the beige house.

"Who is this?" Michael wonders, a ripple of both excitement and apprehension unsettling his usually composed demeanor. "Someone new?" The very idea stirs something in him, a dangerous cocktail of anticipation and darker desires. In a world where he prides himself on knowing every face and detail, this unexpected enigma exhilarates him, calling to the hunter within. As she waved and smiled, Michael's eyes darted from detail to chilling detail: the way her red lipstick seemed to be applied just for him, inviting yet forbidding; her high heels, a clear display of elegance that felt deliberately intentional; her hair, perfectly styled as if each strand was part of an elaborate trap. Everything about her was mysteriously perfect, too refined for everyday life. She must be going somewhere special, he thought, pretending to sort mail while glancing up at her slightly bent over watering a small plant on her steps.

The focus of his gaze, however, was her eyes. They held a depth that both thrilled and unnerved him, evoking a sensation that was less like typical attraction and more like a dark, clawing need. It was an obsession, an unspoken promise of something both divine and dangerous. As he took in her allure, he felt the grip of a desperate, all-consuming yearning, one that edged dangerously close to the boundaries of his tightly wound self-control.

Standing tall and slender, her long blonde hair cascading like a golden waterfall, she meets his gaze with her piercing blue eyes, windows into a world he desperately wants to infiltrate. Michael feels his heart rev into overdrive. "Just my type," he thinks, though the thought is an understatement; it's as if she's been crafted from the darkest corners of his desires. He wipes the sweat pouring from his forehead, his shades now completely fogged up.

His mind isn't just distracted; it's seized, captivated by an almost predatory yearning. It's as though every cell in his body screams for her, a scream that drowns out reason, ethics, and whatever humanity he has left.

He tries to shake the feeling, telling himself that he has work to do. He knows that he shouldn't act on these thoughts, but sometimes it's hard to control the darkness inside him.

Staring back at the woman who waves to him, Michael suddenly feels like he's yanked back in time as if flipping through the worn pages of an old book flooded with memories that are both comforting and painful. He's a lonely 10-year-old kid again, eating lunch alone while everyone else plays. Back then, his mom was his best friend, his only friend. But then Joyce happened. She was the daughter of a single mom, pretty rare in their neighborhood, all the grown men at school seemed to trip over themselves when her mom showed up to drop off Joyce or attend school meetings, always dressed beautifully. One day Joyce broke the rules and sat with him during lunch, talking like they were old friends. She was the prettiest girl he'd ever seen and she seemed okay with him, just as he was. That memory hits him hard now, making him wonder about this new woman, and how his life ended up so twisted.

 He felt an unbelievable rush of luck that day when he was 10 years old, the most beautiful girl he'd ever laid eyes on had no reservations about his loner status. For a moment, life felt different, almost normal, and it was intoxicating.

Even now, as his eyes meet those of this mysterious new woman, the memory of that day with Joyce sears through him; this was the first time his mind drifted back to that fateful day when Joyce had entered his life. He had felt a sense of belonging with her like he had finally found someone who understood him. But as with everything in his life, it was short-lived.

CHAPTER THREE

The woman went back inside taking one last look and smiling before closing the door. Michael shook his head to clear the memories from his mind and refocused on the task at hand, scanning the houses for any mail deliveries he needed to make. He walked his route placing every letter perfectly in the mailbox it belonged and closing it. The day was exhausting. As Michael drove off, memories of the blonde-haired woman lingered in his mind. He couldn't shake the feeling that he had seen her before, and he found himself glancing back at the house as he drove away. It was hard to explain the sudden infatuation he felt for her, but he couldn't deny the pull he felt towards the blonde-haired blue-eyed beauty in the beige house and red dress, like a deeper connection.

After his workday ended, The mailman locked himself in his small apartment. The place was simple, with just a bed, a dresser, and a tiny kitchen. Michael didn't mind the lack of decoration or furniture; it gave him the sense of control, order, and simplicity that he craved. He washed his hands carefully, like he always did, getting rid of the day. He sat at his computer, the screen lighting up his face. He read articles about serial killers and crime, subjects he was deeply interested in but never talked about. To others, it would be a red flag, a warning sign. He was sure people would think it was weird. He checked his social media. No new messages, or notifications. That didn't surprise him; He had always been too focused on his mother and his OCD tendencies to develop any real relationships. But things were changing. Lately, he found himself looking forward to seeing certain women along his mail route. Especially the woman in the beige house she was always on his mind, especially now, lying in bed. Michael couldn't explain the feeling. He wasn't sure what he would say to her, or how he would even start a conversation, but he felt like he had to try. He wanted to talk to her, to be around her. But another part of him, a warning voice in his head, told him it was a bad idea. He knew the kind of attention it could bring, He didn't want to scare her away or do anything to ruin his job and he couldn't afford to mess up, Not now. Instead, he settled for watching her from a distance, studying her movements, and memorizing her address to never miss a letter that was to be delivered there.

CHAPTER FOUR

One night, After a long day of delivering mail, Michael grew restless. He felt like he was suffocating in his small apartment, and he needed to get out. Michael's mind was a storm, restless and unpredictable, swirling around the memory of the mysterious woman in the beige house. She's become the magnet his thoughts can't resist, pulling him into a whirlpool of lust and wonder. His chest tightens with each passing minute, the digital clock on his nightstand ticking away like a countdown to an unknown event.

He decided to take a walk around the block, hoping that some fresh air would clear his head. He put on his coat and gloves, double-checked that his apartment was locked, and stepped out into the chilly night. With both hands in his coat pockets, he walks aimlessly, his mind on autopilot, not noticing the familiarity of the streets beneath the dim glow of the streetlights. It's as if some invisible force has taken control of his feet, leading him through a series of turns and directions only to deposit him at a singular destination.

He stops.

His eyes widen, and like sipping a cup of coffee he's suddenly super awake and aware. He's standing in front of the beige house. The realization washes over him like a cold shower, snapping him back into the reality he'd been trying to escape. He stands there, caught in the web of fate or coincidence, the line between the two now dangerously thin.

 Michael looks around to make sure no one is watching, and then he can't resist the urge to take a closer look, to know more about this new woman. With a glance, he moves toward the beige house, peering through a side window being careful not to touch the glass. "It seems empty" he thought, she must be sleeping. He feels a sense of excitement building within him, and he knows he can't just walk away now.

Michael sees an opening and moves towards the backyard walking calmly, blending in as if he's just another neighbor. He had come this far and was determined to get a glimpse of the tall, beautiful woman. His eyes feel heavy, his blood thick as the pull towards her has him in a trance. Sliding through the open gate in the backyard, He reaches for the back door handle. Then he pauses before touching it. Hand hovering in the air, Michael takes a deep breath and tries to calm himself down.

He pulls his hand back, his skin tingling from the thrill. He knows he can't give in to his urges recklessly. Not yet. Not here.

He retreats from the house and hurries back to his small apartment. Walking up the stairs he finds his front door slightly ajar, the lock not fully secure from when he left. "The door's broken again, damn," he says under his breath, continuing to walk in. Annoyed, he scribbles a note to himself to talk to the landlord. But that thought fades away quickly, drowned out by the ocean of his dark cravings. Michael spends the rest of the night lying down, his mind spinning, a storm of conflicting emotions and unfulfilled desires.

While he lay everything but his head under the covers Michael's mind spiralled back to a night ten years ago. It was an unusually empty evening at the local gym, an environment he had always avoided but couldn't resist that night due to the empty parking lot. He had no plans to exercise; he was there for another reason. His eyes locked onto a striking blonde, someone he'd admired from a distance, but never up close, especially not in a near-empty gym. She was in tight yellow yoga pants, moving gracefully towards the locker room. This was it; he had to make his move. He began to speed walk out of sight around some equipment to intercept her by the water fountain making it look coincidental. Pretending to drink he turns around just as she approaches. "Hey?" he tried, stretching his hand toward her in a weak attempt at connection.

"My name's Michael. I'm your new mailman.

You're here often, aren't you?"

She moved around him, contorting her body to dodge his outstretched hand, eyes rolling annoyed. "Not interested," she called over the pounding beat from her headphones as she stepped into the locker room. Embarrassment washed over Michael's face, staining his cheeks as red as a high-end stiletto sole. He could hear her calling out "Vero! Vero, where are you? "As the locker room door closed, Michael stood arms at his side, chin in his chest, eyes looking forward menacingly through his eyebrows. 'Miss Popular must be meeting a friend' he thought, grinding his teeth. 'Time is running out.' Micheal's mind switches like a light now angry at the rejection.

CHAPTER FIVE

Adrenaline surging, unable to resist the pull any longer, He began to speed walk into the locker room opening it slowly to not alert anyone and closing and locking the door behind him. The air felt electric, a blend of his frenzied emotions and the intense atmosphere, as Micheal sneaks around the lockers to where the woman was seated on a bench half-dressed humming a tune. As if she felt a presence she called out.

"Hello? Vero... is that you?"
The woman's voice reverberates through the empty locker room thinking she heard something. Seated in her underwear, she pulls clothes from a gym bag, the nylon fabric rustling with each grab and the sound of her detached headphones still playing her music

sitting next to her. Suddenly, she freezes. Her eyes dart up, meeting an unsettling sight. It's the man she had casually dismissed earlier, now standing at the end of the bench in the girls' locker room. His posture is eerie, hands by his side, chin pressed to his chest, eyes obscured by the shadow of his brow. He looks not just angry, but possessed, as if controlled by some darker force. The air grows heavy, the tension unbearable. Her instincts scream at her: this is not normal, this is not safe. He flew towards her as if he was pushed by a force, his face distorted and demon-like, arms out aggressively rushing the woman slamming her to the floor, his hands wrapped around her neck stealing the breath she would use to scream. He pressed his face against hers as he felt the life exiting through her beautiful blue eyes, the power feeling as if it transferred from her to him his face strained with veins and anger. His knee now soaked with the woman's urine she released uncontrollably. Out of breath himself he stands up but still towering over her lifeless body, his fist clenched. He pulls from his bag a digital camera and takes a photo to capture the moment of dominance as he sighs in pleasurable relief. The mother's struggle for breath could be heard by the woman's ten-year-old daughter peeking through the cracks from her hiding place inside a random locker. The young girl had originally crawled into a locker as a joke, a playful hide-and-seek game that had spiralled into her worst nightmare. Her mother had rushed into the locker room in a state of maternal urgency, driven by the instinctual need to find her missing daughter, Vero. Calling out, frantically searching, she heard her daughter laugh from a locker so she decided to play along and just get dressed while her daughter hid waiting to act surprised and scared, she had been hoping to hear the laughter of her child. But instead, she had found Michael.

"Mommy? Mommy, where are you?" the girl had called out, her voice shaking with fear as she climbed out of the locker.

Michael had slipped into the shower area unnoticed, Draped in shadow, becoming a mere silhouette against the tiled walls. He watched, his breaths shallow and controlled, as the girl scoured the locker area. Her footsteps tapped out a slow disconnected rhythm of desperation as she moved closer to the place where her mother lay unresponsive.

"Mommy, wake up! Wake up, mommy!" the girl had cried, her voice rising in panic.

Michael had held his breath, waiting as the girl edged toward the exit to get help. With each step she took, the strings of Michael's tension wound tighter, like a bow drawn back to its breaking point. The moment she vanished from sight; Michael appeared out of his dark hiding place. Swift as a ghost, he scaled the locker room window, his muscles coiled with a mix of adrenaline and dark exhilaration. Taking a mental snapshot of the scene he left behind, he melted into the night, he knew he wouldn't be able to shake the haunting cries that still seemed to hang in the air, phantom sounds that would follow him long after he had made his harrowing escape.

Now, as Michael lay in bed emotions swirling from the flashback, a growing sense of excitement began to stir within him. He knew that he needed to find another victim soon, or his urges would consume him completely like before. But for now, he had to bide his time and wait for the perfect opportunity. Or was this love at first sight finally and the woman he needed for closure to these nightmare urges and untamed rage? He rolled over on his side to catch whatever sleep he could get from the night.

CHAPTER SIX

Weeks had melted into months, and every day delivering mail felt more and more important, though he couldn't say why. The beige house had turned into a special stop on his daily route, and every quick interaction with her, a glance, a smile, felt like a piece of a puzzle he couldn't help but want to solve.

Michael had seen her numerous times by now, enough to notice the subtleties: the slight tilt of her head, the mysterious sparkle in her eyes, even the graceful way she moved. Each detail built a fire in his chest, an increasing fascination that grew with each passing day. As he got near the beige house, he knew exactly what letters were for her and he had them set aside hoping to focus his attention so he could catch a glimpse of her. One afternoon while Micheal was delivering mail to his favorite beige home, A folded piece of paper rested in her mailbox, he grabbed it and replaced it neatly tucking the bills and junk mail in the box. Michael's eyes widened as he read the note: "Great job, Michael! Your hard work doesn't go unnoticed. I baked some cookies to show my appreciation." His heart swelled; a warmth came over his body as if fueled by an unseen energy source.

Taking a moment to centre himself, he pulled the mail back out, deciding to hand deliver it. Smiling nervously, he assembled the stack of mail, carefully placing her note on top. With every step toward her front door, the nerves tangled themselves into knots, but he wrestled them into submission, managing what he hoped was a confidently casual walk towards her house.

The door creaked open before he even reached it, and there she was. Her face lit up with a bright smile as if she had been waiting just for him. She extended a plate filled with golden cookies toward Michael, their aroma filling the air with a blend of sugar, love, and chocolate.

"Hi there, I'm Veronica," she greeted him. "I just wanted to thank you for being such a reliable mailman. Here, have a cookie."

Michael felt his universe go silent as he accepted the cookie, savoring the feeling of her fingers against his as she handed it to him. There was something about her that made him feel both excited and uneasy at the same time. He scrambled mentally for a response.

"I appreciate the gesture, Veronica, but job rules say no eating," he said, instantly wishing he'd framed it differently.

"Then maybe you could try them later? We could even meet for coffee to discuss your culinary critique," Veronica offered, her smile tinged with a playful allure. A pulse of excitement jolted through Michael. Was this happening?

"I'd love that," he managed to say, concealing the thrill that surged within him.

As he walked back to his mail truck, Michael couldn't stop thinking about Veronica. He felt like he had finally found someone who understood his awkwardness, someone who he could connect with effortlessly. But something about her made him feel uneasy, and he couldn't quite put his finger on it.

Just as he settled into his seat, absorbed in the next set of addresses on his route, a loud knock on the window jolted him. Heart leaping into his throat, he turned to see Veronica's face inches from the glass.

"I forgot to give you my number in case you need anything," she said, slipping a piece of paper through the window.

"Thanks, Veronica. I appreciate it," Michael said, his mind racing with possibilities.

Veronica shot him one last smile before heading back to her house. Michael stayed parked for a bit, trying to wrap his head around the whole encounter. Sure, he was excited about the prospect of seeing her again and tasting those cookies, but he couldn't shake off some nagging doubts. He was well into middle age, while she was much younger.

"Why would she be interested in me?" he thought. "Does she think I've got money, or does she have some weird fantasy about older guys?" The questions churned in his mind, adding a layer of unease to his excitement. She was way too young for him, so what was going on? That thought loomed large in Michael's mind casting a shadow over his excitement. The question poked at Michael for the rest of his shift, but deep down, he couldn't shake the hope that maybe, just maybe, she was just really into him and genuine in her interest. On the way home in his small car after the day's intriguing encounter with Veronica, Michael felt unusually at ease as he pulled into his apartment's parking lot. But as he began climbing the stairway to his unit, he froze. Across the dimly lit lot, he spotted a silhouette of a figure shrouded in darkness, seemingly watching him. His heart accelerated. Was he being followed? He squinted, attempting to decipher any facial features, but the veil of night concealed the figure's identity. The unsettling sensation of being watched tingled down his spine.

Summoning his courage, Michael slowly walked back to the parking lot and approached the figure with cautious steps. Each footfall echoed in his ears, amplifying the drumming of his heartbeat. But as he drew near, the tension broke, his so-called stalker morphed into the innocent shape of a tree, its shadow mimicking a human form in the parking lot's poor lighting.

Not entirely convinced, he walked further down the street. His eyes darted from corner to corner, scanning the darkened alleyways and concealed spaces. Yet, there was no one to be found. Had his imagination gotten the best of him, or was this a warning signal, the beginning of something he couldn't yet fathom?

His heart still racing, Michael climbed the remaining steps to his apartment, glancing back one final time at the parking lot, now seemingly innocent but still tinged with the afterglow of his unsettling suspicion. He fumbled with his keys; their jangling sound was unnaturally loud in the quiet hallway.

Finally, inside, he locked the door behind him and paused, listening intently. Silence. The only sound was the distant hum of the town beyond his walls. For a moment, he allowed himself to breathe, to hope that his mind had simply been playing tricks on him.

But as he turned to move further into the apartment, a flicker of doubt flew into his brain. Could it have been just a tree, a mere shadow? Or was it a sinister prelude, a warning he was too frightened to heed?

Michael went about his nightly routine, but that unsettling feeling clawed at the back of his mind, refusing to be shaken off. The tree, the shadow,

Veronica's sudden and unexplainable interest, all these pieces floated in a mental jigsaw puzzle that refused to come together.

And as he lay in bed that night, staring up at the ceiling, the darkness in the room seemed heavier, almost expectant. Michael closed his eyes, hoping to escape into the relief of sleep. But behind his eyelids, the day's events replayed like a haunting melody, punctuated by the unsettling notion that he was missing something crucial, something that lay just beyond the reach of his understanding.

As he finally drifted off into an uneasy slumber, His dreams carried the same unnerving thoughts: Had he become the unsuspecting star of a drama whose script he did not yet fully comprehend? And what role did Veronica play in all of this, that young enigma who had so suddenly stepped onto his stage stirring a complex blend of dark impulses and newfound hope? Could she be the one person who made him feel genuinely secure in this world? Maybe this was the real thing, true love, or love at first sight as they say. The shadow now seemed almost like a maternal spirit, guiding Michael on what needed to be done.

In the dead of night, these questions swirled in the darkness around him, his usual urges now hidden in the dark corners of his mind, as elusive as the shadow in the parking lot.

CHAPTER SEVEN

A few days later, Michael gathered the courage to text her. "Tried your cookies, they're incredible! Makes me want another taste of what you can do." "really" she texted back followed by a thinking and heart emoji. Micheal now oozing confidence responds "Next cookout I'm inviting you, let me know if you can cum?" A typo turned "come" into "cum," but instead of panicking, he sent the message anyway. To his relief, she responded warmly. "Haha, glad you enjoyed them! I can't wait for you to try more of my 'special deliveries.'"
Over time their texts became more frequent and flirtatious. Sometimes they were innocent enough, updates about mail deliveries or the weather, but other times they hinted at something more.

"You've got a 'package' waiting," he'd text, and

she'd reply, "I hope it's as special as the last one."

He even found time during his route to stop by her place, no longer just a mailman but a welcomed guest. They'd share quick chats and occasional cups of tea. Each visit deepened his affection for her and, he hoped, her interest in him. Yet, amid the warm smiles and inviting glances, Something was off, Micheal felt like he was trying to show he liked her for weeks and he was still just a friend, deep down he started wanting to be more. He wasn't sure if she liked him but he knew there was a hidden layer to their growing friendship, one he couldn't quite figure out, clouded perhaps by his complicated feelings and a history he couldn't fully recall.

 On one of his rare days off, instead of enjoying the nice California weather. Micheal found himself pacing the worn carpet of his dimly lit apartment, his thoughts only about Veronica. For weeks, he'd texted and seen her on his mail route, but now, a new sensation eclipsed his darker urges: genuine attraction. He decided he needed to tell her how he felt if he wished to dive into the layers of her life, to hear her laughter, and to witness the authentic smile that could only come from shared joy. The looming possibility of rejection turned his palms sweaty, Leaving him uneasy and anxious. But he knew the time had come to finally be honest about his feelings. Taking a deep breath, he made up his mind: he would tell her how he felt, no matter what happened.

Micheal replayed every moment he had seen her on his mail route from the day they met, each encountering a chapter in an unfolding story. Now, Michael felt compelled to turn the page, to find out if her feelings mirrored his own. With newfound determination, he decided that tomorrow would be the day he'd finally reveal his emotions to her.

The day to tell her came, and his route that day was as ordinary as ever. Michael found himself hoping for some kind of distraction, maybe a loose dog or a confrontational customer, anything to take his mind off the butterflies in his stomach. But he realized he needed to face this now. It couldn't wait, it was better to get it over with to rip the Band-Aid off. The anticipation was clouding his focus on the job, and he only had a few minutes to spare on his route. He decided he would go there first. Michael, known for his punctuality, felt the pressure of the ticking clock. He revved the engine of the mail truck, making hasty turns and speeding recklessly down the roads as he neared the familiar beige house. He felt like today was the day to take control of his emotions and tell her how he felt.

Just as he thought he was about to get his moment; the flashing lights of a police car caught his eye in the rearview mirror. Cursing softly, he pulled the truck over to the side of the road, feeling like fate itself was trying to keep him away from Veronica for fear he might still want to dominate her.

The police officer, a woman with short black hair and ocean-blue eyes, took her time getting out of the car. Michael's eyes met those of the officer, a flicker of recognition crossing his mind. She seemed familiar, yet he couldn't quite pinpoint where he'd seen her before.

"Good morning, sir. Do you know why I pulled you over?" the officer asked in a stern tone of authority. Michael shook his head, feeling a growing sense of unease in the pit of his stomach.

"I forgot to deliver your package on time," he said trying to lighten the mood.

"You were driving recklessly and endangering other drivers on the road. And in a fucking mail truck! License and registration, please," the officer said, her eyes fixed on him.

Michael fumbled for his license and registration, his hands shaking with nerves. As he handed the documents over, the officer glanced at his license and her eyes widened in recognition.

"Michael? Michael Ross?" she said, Her tone softened remarkably.

Michael looked up, startled. It suddenly clicked, and he realized who the officer was. This was Joyce, his childhood confidante and friend from school. The one girl who had always accepted him, quirks and all sitting with Micheal every day at lunch. They'd lost touch years ago.

"Joyce?" he said, his voice hoarse. "Is that you?"

Joyce nodded, a small smile playing at the corners of her mouth. "It's been a long time, Michael. How have you been?"

Relief washed over him like a warm summer rain. If anyone could understand him, it was Joyce. "I've been good, all things considered. How about you? You're a police officer now? And your hair, it's not blonde anymore?

"I have changed Michael, I had to after... she shook her head "Look a lot has changed you should understand that"

She paused, her eyes turning distant, as though revisiting painful memories or an unspoken Trama.

She refocused, Joyces smile now faded, replaced by a stern, almost sad expression.

"I have a job to do, Michael. I'm a police officer now. And I have to say, your driving today was reckless and dangerous. I could have to ticket you, or worse, take you in," her voice breaking tears welled in her eyes as she spoke, and Michael felt his own emotions bubbling over. They had been through so much together.

He stepped out of the truck, pulling her into a tight hug. "I'm so sorry, Joyce," he choked out, "I should have stayed I know" he said both of them now in tears. His voice tinged with regret and years of unspoken words. "I should have looked for you. We've lost so much time."Pushing him back, her expression grew stern, yet her eyes remained moist.

"You left," she said "I stayed, who could have imagined all that happened, Mike"

As Michael looked into Joyce's eyes, memories surged back like a tidal wave crashing on the shores of his mind. He remembered being a kid, super excited to go to Joyce's birthday party. His mother said she would accompany him, but she fell ill the day before, grounding her to the bed. After a lot of begging, his dad finally said he'd drop him off, just so he could get back to his football game. Micheal's mom had always had a sharp eye for details. She had noticed the magnetic charm of Joyce's mom during quick conversations the two women had at the grocery store and casual waves at the school drop-offs for the kids. "Be quick, love, you don't want to miss the game," she had told her husband, her voice weak from illness. "And have fun, Michael."

When they pulled up to Joyce's house, decked out for a birthday bash, Michael's dad was instantly taken by Joyce's mom, who stood on the porch looking like something out of a dream. No other cars were in sight; it appeared that they were the only guests. He fixed his face and clothes before walking up. The party vibe felt down; everything was set up for a big crowd, but it was just the four of them. Joyce's mom had gone all out for this party, but the empty yard told a different story. It was a tough truth to face: her daughter Joyce and Michael were the kids no one wanted to hang out with. "Is anyone else coming?" Michael's father said playfully, attempting humour that only served to fracture Joyce's mother's fragile composure. She broke down crying, her sobs filling the air with an unbearable heaviness. Sensing her vulnerability, Michael's father quickly sent the children outside with bubbles and art supplies. He turned his attention back to Joyce's mother, comforting her with whispered affirmations. As the minutes stretched into wine-filled hours, the invisible thread of temptation was too much to resist, the two adults becoming a whirlpool of desire and regret, and before they knew it, they were sharing a secret kiss in a secluded bedroom.

Meanwhile, Michael's mother was at home, uneasy and restless in bed, stuck to a replaying bad feeling that kept tugging at her sanity. Glancing at the clock and seeing the game had ended, her anxiety ramped up. Thoughts of Joyce's attractive mom didn't help. When she heard about an accident along the way to Joyce's house, it gave her the push she needed to get out of bed and go check things out. Without a second thought, she slipped into her shoes and drove off, her heart pounding in sync with the car's tires on the road.

Arriving at the house, her eyes met only her husband's car and the children outside. A volatile cocktail of jealousy and rage boiled within her as she rushed past Michael and Joyce's innocent, smiling face in the yard. When she made it to the living room, she didn't see anyone, just party decorations and some empty wine glasses. Unhinged, she snatched a knife from the birthday cake on the kitchen counter and moved with grim purpose toward the bedroom. The telltale sounds of laughter and intimacy poured from behind the door. In a blaze of fiery anger, she burst into the room, brandishing the knife as she screamed, "How could you do this to me, to us, to our family!?" The two startled lovers separated in an instant, their faces masks of guilt and shock. And there, in the doorway, stood Michael, who had followed his mother, his young eyes absorbing a scene that would fracture his understanding of love, fidelity, and family forever.

Michael looked on in horror, tears streaming down his face as he witnessed the destruction of his family. In the heat of the moment, he watched as his mother jumped onto the bed, straddling Joyce's mom. She plunged a long knife repeatedly into Joyce's mom's chest. Each stab released bursts of red-like paint, colouring and splattering both of them as if they bathed in it like red water. Michael's dad jumped up, making a beeline for the door to get Michael who stood frozen, eyes wide. Overall the chaos, he heard his mom's angry shout, "You think just because you're pretty, you get everything?!"She then noticed his dad trying to exit the room. Swiftly turning and jumping off the bed, she ran toward him and grabbed him from behind. Using the same long knife she pulled from the girl's mom, she gave him three hard stabs in the neck, and he dropped down, falling right at her son Michael's feet. A spray of fresh blood from his father's neck splashed all over Michael, but all he saw was his mother's face, twisted in anger, almost monster-like.

When her rage died down, Michael's mom held him close, both covered in colorful splatters. She whispered deeply into his ear, "Micheal, they're all devilish homewreckers, especially the ones with blond hair and blue eyes. They think they can have it all!" Her eyes looked wide and deranged holding Michael's body covered in his own dad's blood "I love you so much" she whispered as sirens approached the house neighbors hearing the craziness and calling the cops. Michael never forgot that moment, and neither did Joyce. Though she never stepped inside to witness the chaotic scene, she did see Michael's mother emerge from the house, flanked by police officers, her face and clothes stained with red. Only her eyes were visible, wide and unsettling. Following behind were stretchers carrying her mother and Michael's father, their lifeless forms concealed under blood-stained sheets. The paramedics shook their heads in disbelief, a wordless confirmation of the tragedy that had just unfolded.

In that sea of chaos, Joyce felt unseen until a compassionate female police officer approached her in the front yard, taking her hand. It was an act of kindness that deeply moved Joyce and planted the seed of her future career in law enforcement. It was also that fateful day that set Michael on his life path, a path defined by the darkness he had witnessed.

As the memory began to fade, Michael was abruptly pulled back into the present. He looked into Joyce's eyes and felt a mix of guilt and sadness. Their shared past, the haunting memories he'd spent years trying to bury, had been dredged up in that single moment of recognition

"Okay, Michael. I'll let you off with a warning this time. But be careful on the road. And we should catch up sometime soon; it's been too long," Joyce said, handing back his license and registration with a knowing smile. "Oh no, not a warning," Michael replied, his eyes glistening with emotion. A lot of history lay between them, and now that Joyce was back in town and as a cop, no less there was no way they could avoid reconnecting.

"I can't believe you're here."

"I know," Joyce said softly, her eyes meeting his. Michael turned the key, revving up the mail truck's engine. "Be careful out there."

"If you need me, call me," Joyce said, biting her lip as she handed him a business card.

"I think I'll just call 911 if I want to see you," Michael retorted, the tension lifting a bit.

"Same, same," Joyce chuckled, watching as he drove off.

As Michael drove away from his surprising encounter with Joyce, her beauty was what surprised him most. It was hard to believe she was back in town, and as a police officer no less. He was now thinking maybe this was destiny at play. His eyes flicked to the rearview mirror one last time before focusing on the road ahead, toward Veronica's house. Pulling up in front of the beige charming home, he parked his mail truck and took a deep, steadying breath. It was now or never; he had to tell her how he felt.

Gathering his courage, he walked up the pathway and rang the doorbell, his pulse pounding like a drum solo in a rock concert. The door opened, and there stood Veronica, looking surprised but happy to see him.

"Hey, Michael," she greeted, a warm smile brightening her face.

"Hello, Veronica," Michael replied, struggling to keep his nerves in check. "There's something I've been wanting to tell you."

Intrigue crossed her face. "Oh?"

"I know we haven't had the chance to get to know each other," Michael went on, "but for some reason, I can't stop thinking about you. There's just something about you that pulls me in. Would you be interested in going out with me sometime?"

Veronica looked shocked for a second, and Michael's heart sank, bracing himself for rejection. But then her lips curved into a smile that felt like the morning sun breaking through a night of darkness.

"I'd like that, Michael," she responded, delight evident in her voice. "I've noticed you on your route for a while now and wondered when you'd finally gather the courage to ask me out."

A wave of relief washed over Michael, and he grinned, his eyes twinkling with newfound hope.

"Awesome," he exclaimed. "How about dinner on Friday night?" Veronica nodded, her smile undiminished.

"I'd love to," she confirmed.

As Michael walked back to his truck, heart lighter and step quicker, his mood was elevated to new highs and maybe just maybe life was aligning in his favor.

CHAPTER EIGHT

Michael drove, finishing his day when he left Veronica's house, his mind racing with thoughts of their upcoming date on Friday night. His body felt both nervous and excited still buzzing with the thrill of it. He couldn't wait for Friday night when they had made plans for their date. Little did he know that Veronica was watching him as he drove away, a sly smile on her face.

When he arrived home that night, He walked around his room, unsure of what to do with himself, his thoughts bouncing between preparing the room for a romantic evening with Veronica or a more violent scenario involving dominance and her demise. He had never felt this way about anyone before, the way her smile lit up her face and the sound of her laughter made his heart shake.

A sense of anticipation for Friday bubbled up within him, hard to ignore. So much so that he began to prepare his room for their date already. He put fresh sheets on the bed, placed some candles, and laid out some wine and glasses. But as he worked, he found himself fighting the urge to prepare his room for something else entirely. His mind wandered to thoughts of dominating Veronica, of making her submit to him in every way possible. He pushed the thoughts away, reminding himself that he didn't want to hurt her. He just wanted to make her happy.

Even the hum of the car seemed to resonate with the rhythm of his heartbeat. Her eyes, and her laughter; danced around his thoughts, making it hard to focus on anything else. Yet, in the shadows of his mind, lurked something more sinister. As he thought of their conversation a flash that he might have caught a brief glimpse of Veronica's reflection in his rearview mirror. Her expression held a hint of mischief, but was it just his imagination?

Inside his apartment, Michael felt a restless energy. The duel of contrasting emotions was playing out before him, in the form of his preparations. He wanted this date to be perfect, hence the wine and the fresh sheets. But an undercurrent of darker desires threatened to surface desires that spoke of control and domination. Desires he hadn't allowed himself to feel in a long while. The thoughts were unwelcome, especially now that he had a genuine chance with someone as magnetic as Veronica. She deserved respect, not the stormy impulses that threatened to overtake him.

Realizing he needed a break from his spiralling thoughts, Michael decided to call up Joyce. It had been a few days now since the traffic stop, and maybe reconnecting with a part of his past would help ground him.

Joyce's voice, a familiar tone from a seemingly different lifetime, held a note of surprise. "Michael? It's been ages."

"Yeah, too long. Fancy catching up over a drink?" he asked.

"You're lucky… it's my day off, and catching up sounds good," Joyce agreed, and they settled on a local bar.

Michael stepped into the dimly lit bar, the hum of quiet conversations and clinking glasses offering a backdrop to his growing unease. The familiar face of Joyce, sitting at a corner table, beckoned him over. While their histories were intertwined, they'd grown apart, and tonight, the undercurrents of their past threatened to surface. She was a beacon of law, he was more than a killer he was the shadow that existed beyond it.

"Michael," she said warmly, rising to hug him. As they embraced, he felt the simmering guilt, the weight of countless secrets concealed behind his every action. They settled into a rhythm, speaking of old memories and the paths their lives had taken. Yet, with every sip of alcohol, the boundaries began to blur, washing away the caution that once governed his every move.

The night wore on, and under the intoxication, their worlds collided in unexpected ways. Michael, drawn by the magnetic pull of Joyce's eyes, leaned in. Their lips met, and in that suspended moment, time seemed to halt. But as they separated, a chilling realization settled over him. The depth of emotion he felt in that kiss was foreign, a divergence from the calculated detachment he maintained with his victims.

Conflicted and overwhelmed, Michael downed the remainder of his drink, the weight of the night's revelations heavy on his shoulders. The night was drawing to an end, and with it, the complexities of their shared past threatened to pull them both under. Michael drove home, his mind spinning with mixed feelings. The echo of his mother's voice reverberated through his thoughts, a stark warning from behind the cold prison glass that separated her from the world before she died. "Never fall into the trap of a woman's beauty, Michael. It's a Venus flower, set only to trap and destroy you." He tried to brush it off, blaming the alcohol for messing with his head. The thought was as unsettling as it was inevitable: the urge all too familiar, he wanted to kill Joyce. A notion that had never before entered his mind. He quickly blamed it on his new emotions towards Veronica. He would never hurt Joyce and was torn between his feelings for Veronica and his compulsion to harm her. That was enough for him to know that Veronica must go to cure his urge.

His keys jingled in the hallway unlocking his apartment door, each metallic click sounding like a countdown to something sinister. He stepped in and looked around. The place felt different now as if the walls knew what he was thinking. He cleared the romantic stuff he'd put out earlier, the wine glasses, the candles. They didn't belong in this story anymore.

Lying in bed, he knew he was at a crossroads. He invited back his dark urge to harm Veronica. She was different from Joyce, and in his mind, that made it okay. But could he go through with it? The question was eating at him.

His eyes fell on the calendar hanging on the wall. Friday was marked in red. It felt like a deadline, the day everything would come to a head. It wasn't long now. Sleep wouldn't touch him for days.

When Friday arrived, Michael sat on his couch, fidgeting and restless. All week he'd been getting ready for tonight, but now, something didn't sit right. The dark urge to harm Veronica was growing, fighting for room in his mind. Shaking his head, he tried to keep those thoughts at bay and focus on doing everything right on the date ahead.

As Michael buttoned up his shirt for the date, a mix of excitement and apprehension filled him. The reality sank in that this would be the last time he'd see Veronica alive, he was now so used to seeing her every day on his mail route that the visits made him feel drawn to her. He felt like he was in a suspenseful movie, where he played both the predator and the love interest.

As Michael arrived at Veronica's doorstep, he took a deep breath and tried to calm his nerves. He knocked on the door, and when Veronica answered, he was taken aback by how beautiful she looked. She smiled at him, and he felt like he was on top of the world.

Once they arrived at the restaurant, he was surprised when Veronica reached over to hold his hand. The room buzzed with the chatter of other diners; so many conversations happening around him that he couldn't focus on any. But one thing was for sure the aroma of Asian cuisine made his stomach growl, an unsettling normality in what he knew was an abnormal night.

CHAPTER NINE

As Michael and Veronica sat at their table, savoring their meals, a Latina's voice from across the restaurant punctured the atmosphere. "Vero, is that you?" she shouted towards their table.

Veronica turned, her eyes lighting up as she recognized an old friend from childhood. While they caught up with laughter and memories, Michael felt a cold, electric shiver go through him. That name. 'Vero.' He'd heard it before, but where?

Suddenly, it slammed into him like a runaway train. He remembered the woman he had killed in the locker room and the name she had called out before she died. It was "Vero!". She wasn't looking for her friend in the locker room that day, she was looking for her daughter. Michael felt his stomach drop as Veronica's old friend said, "I'm sorry for what happened to your mother."

His heart exploded in his chest. Could it be? Was this the same Vero? The daughter of the woman he'd snuffed out so many years ago? His dinner suddenly tasted like ashes, and every glance he gave Veronica seemed filled with deadly tension. This was what he felt before his instincts fine-tuned the real reason he was so sceptical before.

"So, how did you lose your mother?" Michael tried to sound casual, but his voice shook.

"Violently," she answered, her eyes narrowing as she twisted spaghetti around her fork. Her expression was no longer that of a friendly date.

Earlier, while Michael was getting ready for this date, he had been wrestling with darker desires, the urge to harm lurking in the background. He even went as far as adding plastic gloves and a mask to his outfit stashed away just in case.

What he had never imagined was Veronica had been prepping too, but not with dinner or romance in mind. She had been meticulously setting up her plan as she always did. This wasn't the first time she'd taken down mailmen in the hunt for her mother's killer, but none had made her doubt like Michael did. His charm was unsettling, making her second-guess her once unshakable convictions.

She'd been watching him for weeks, trying to spot any signs that he was the savage she was convinced had killed her mother. Yet, he had shown none. She had thought she would seize the first opportunity to exact her revenge, but now, she found herself hesitating. Her cover, she feared, might already be blown, and the awful truth was, she wasn't completely certain Michael was the man she'd been hunting.

The air between them thickened, both teetering on the edge of a cliff, both with secrets that could push the other over. The night was far from over, and the air was charged with a tension that promised an explosive end. Who would make the first move? Both of their eyes locked in on each other undressing the outer layers they showed in the very beginning.

As she answered violently Michael's eyes locked onto Veronica's, his face transforming, the charm that had so far defined the evening evaporating in an instant. It was as if they had both silently acknowledged that the pleasantries were over. They were in a high-stakes game now, a deadly dance neither could back out of.

"What a tragedy. She must have been so beautiful," Michael said, his voice laced with a chilling undertone. He brought his coffee cup to his lips, blowing off the steam as if trying to cool down the boiling tension between them.

Veronica felt her heart slam against her ribcage. Something in Michael had shifted; it was like watching a curtain rise, revealing a much darker stage. Could this man be the monster she had been hunting, the killer who haunted her nightmares? She had been mistaken before; after all, her only memory from that horrific day was a figure with glasses carrying a post office bag. But something about Michael resonated with her and made her recall that terrible night at the gym with her mother.

She felt a new urgency, a creeping fear that Michael was onto her. If he was the man from her past, then every second she hesitated put her at risk. Her plan wasn't fully formed yet, but time was a luxury she could no longer afford. She needed to act, and she needed to act fast.

CHAPTER TEN

The restaurant around them blurred into a backdrop, a mere setting for the psychological thriller they were both enacting. Words were pointless now; their eyes carried conversations, accusations, and confessions. The stakes were not clear: something was different this time. She felt like she was connected to this man possibly through that night of tragedy with her mother at the gym. She felt a growing suspicion that he was onto her like he knew what she was planning. She tried to hide her unease and continue the conversation, but her mind was already racing with thoughts of how to evade suspicion. She was still identifying who he was, her plan for revenge not fully together yet. But if he was the man, she would have to get prepared quickly as he would now be on to her for sure. As they finished up their dinner and said their goodbyes, Veronica noticed that Michael was watching and analyzing her every move. She made an excuse to leave the restaurant early, looking back in her rearview mirror at a waving Michael in the parking lot as she drove away, running every red light and quickly making her way back to her house. Once inside, she immediately locked the door and checked her phone for any missed calls or messages. Breathing a sigh of relief, she realized that Michael had not caught on to her plan. But she couldn't let her guard down just yet. As she walked to her backdoor to check the lock there was Michael. He was already in her kitchen standing in the darkness his arms at his side, chin in his chest, eyes looking forward menacingly through his eyebrows. Her mind freezes as she sees his silhouette before reaching for the light. When it came on she was surprised by his monster-like face flying towards her.

Fear gripped her, and instinctively, she backed away from his advance, stumbling over a chair and falling to the floor. She reached out for something, anything to defend herself. Her hand landed on a small knife that she had left on the counter earlier. In the haze of panic, her mind registered danger and fight or flight kicked in. Gripping it tightly, she pointed it towards Michael, trying to mimic the stance of self-defence. A strange mix of confusion and some amusement flickered in Michael's eyes as he observed Veronica clutching the small knife as her weapon. The absurdity of the situation almost broke through his dark intentions, and a slight smirk tugged at the corners of his lips. Veronica, fueled by adrenaline and knowing that her life was in imminent danger, lunged forward, wildly swinging the knife at Michael. She darted through her house, weaving between furniture and knocking over objects in her path, creating a chaotic scene reminiscent of a horror movie.

Michael, caught off guard by Veronica's unexpected resistance, stumbled backwards, evading the clumsy attacks of the small knife but filled with blood-boiling rage and desire now. He found himself caught in the surreal dance of pursuit and evasion; the seriousness of his intentions was momentarily overshadowed by the absurdity of the chase. Vero created enough space between them with her attack to run towards the stairs, her intention to get to the bedroom where she had been preparing to fight with Micheal when the time was right. As Veronica's desperate escape continued, she ran up the stairs knocking over a small bookshelf and sliding it down the stairs towards Micheal slowing him down as it hit his legs. When she reached the bedroom at the end of the hallway, her mind scrambled for the key to the case by her bed that held her 12-gauge pump action shotgun she readied and loaded before she went out with Michael for this very moment.

Spotting the key on a nearby shelf, she snatched it up, believing to have time to open the case in the heat of the moment. Her sweaty hands fumbling with the key as she put it in the lock and twisted, looking back at the door knowing Michael would burst in at any moment she cracked the case open and she reached for the cold metal of the gun, she felt a python-like squeeze on her neck from behind, effectively stopping her progress. Veronica, now caught in Michael's rear naked choke and pulled off her feet grasp from behind, felt a mix of fear and confusion. Her surroundings became a blur as she blinked rapidly, struggling to regain her composure and losing control of her bladder. He had her in the air, her face straining so full of blood a leech would be jealous. The room seemed to spin around her, and her consciousness wavered. She desperately searched for an escape route but found herself losing control of her body. Her last thoughts are she let her mother down and would suffer the same fate from the same man. Right before she passed out she heard a female voice yell out from downstairs police! as she blacked out. Michael dropped Veronica to the ground recognizing the sound of the cop's voice. He wiped his sweat off his forehead and walked into the hallway to try to explain away the mess and stop her from seeing Veronica in the room unconscious. He ran back down the stairs jumping over the bookshelf and placing his hands in the air. "Whoa! Hotshot! Take it easy" he said with a friendly laugh. "You sweating profusely Michael" Joyce said two hands on her pistol standing in the kitchen Michael used to catch Vero by surprise.

"Where's the girl?" Joyce asked her face as serious as cancer news from a doctor.

"You came here alone Joyce" Michael responded, wiping his face with his shirt and walking towards Joyce checking around for her backup. Joyce now realises the danger she is in. As Michael stood there, wanting to finish his dark frenzy Joyce's presence only intensified his inner struggle. The urge, the insatiable desire for blonde hair and blue eyes, threatened to consume him. He could see it in Joyce's piercing blue eyes and the golden roots of their hair peeking through her new dark hair color. The scent of her hair filled his nostrils, triggering a surge of conflicting emotions within him. Trying to maintain his composure, Michael forced a smile.

"Joyce, I haven't seen Vero. I thought she was supposed to be here," he replied, his voice betraying a hint of unease.
Joyce's eyes narrowed as she studied Michael, sensing something amiss.

"I received a tip about Vero's dangerous activities with mailmen across California, and when I found out you were on a date, I knew I had to investigate," she said, her voice filled with authority.
"What dangerous activities," Micheal asked, confused

at Joyce's presence in the house at all. Joyce hesitated for a moment, her eyes meeting Michael's. Slowly, she lowered her gun and exhaled deeply.

"You need to understand, Michael, Veronica isn't just some random woman you've been dating. She's a serial killer."

Michael felt his stomach churn as Joyce continued.

"She's been travelling from town to town for years now, the same system, she rents a place set out on seducing mailmen and then killing them. She's left a gruesome trail of unsolved cases behind her. I've been tracking her for a while, and it's like she's hunting some kind of twisted vengeance."

Seeing Michael's confused expression, Joyce pulled out her phone and showed him an old newspaper article. It featured Michael, grinning widely, with a headline that read, "Mailman of the Year Awarded to Stockton's Michael." "Your recognition didn't just catch the community's attention, Michael," Joyce said. "It caught hers. Veronica has been focusing on mailmen for a reason." Michael stared at Joyce, trying to absorb the information.

"But why mailmen? What's the connection?"

Joyce sighed, choosing her words carefully. "From what we've gathered, Veronica believes that a mailman killed her mother many years ago. She was young, but she saw something, or thinks she saw something, that led her to this belief. Since then, she's been on a mission, a deranged quest, you could call it. She's trying to find the mailman responsible for her mother's death and exact her form of bloody justice. It's like she's trying to balance the scales but in a horrifically wrong way." Joyce paused, letting the magnitude of her revelation sink in. "And Michael you were almost her next victim."

Before Michael could process everything Joyce had said the bedroom door slowly creaked open. The dim light of the hallway framed Veronica, her face twisted in fury and desperation, holding a shotgun that was almost too large for her frame. The look in her eyes was pure evil, and Michael felt a chill go through him.

As Veronica aimed the shotgun at them, her intent deadly clear, Joyce, with lightning reflexes, pulled out her sidearm. But Veronica was quick too. Just as she was about to squeeze the trigger, Joyce's bullet found its mark, hitting Veronica's shoulder. The shotgun blast went wild, the deafening sound filling the room, scattering pellets that hit Joyce's arm and buried themselves in the wall.

Veronica screamed in pain and shock, dropping her weapon as she staggered back. The severity of her wound was evident by the blood staining her clothes. Seizing the moment, Michael lunged forward, snatching up the fallen shotgun. With adrenaline-fueled determination, he aimed and fired at Veronica's legs. The spread of the shot was devastating, tearing through flesh and bone. Joyce, having taken cover, emerged nursing her bleeding arm, her face a mask of pain and determination. The room was filled with the overpowering scent of gunpowder and blood.

With Veronica squirming on the floor, Michael, his face contorted with a rage she had awoken, he picked up the small knife off the counter. He advanced on her, his intentions clear. Joyce, realizing what was about to unfold, cried out, too weak to break through Michael's frenzied state. The climax of Vero's and Michael's intertwined fates was playing out and the showdown was about to happen. Micheal lifted Vero in the air by her neck with one hand. He now looked super strong from rage at the sight of blood.

Joyce looked on in horror as Michael slid the small knife into Vero, a look of sexual pleasure on his face accompanied by a nut stain in his cargo pants. He drops the knife and wipes blood across his tongue, picking up the shotgun and turning to where Joyce is lying holding her arm.

Joyce's eyes widened; her realization was too late. Michael, torn between his love for her and the compulsion that threatened to consume him, whispered, "I'm sorry, Joyce he said his voice much deeper and scarier. "That day, your birthday! made me like this."

A moment of deafening silence filled the room as their eyes locked, the weight of their shared history and childhood memories hanging in the air. Joyce, now considering Micheal might be the guy that Vero had been looking for all along, the Mailman serial killer she said took her mother. Michael's grip tightened, his finger inching towards the trigger.

Just as he prepared to pull the trigger, the distant sound of police sirens began to wail. Realizing time was against him, Michael looked at Joyce one last time.

"You may run, but you can't escape yourself," she said before her eyes rolled back and she passed out.

Hearing the sirens grow louder, Michael knew he had only seconds to spare. He dropped the shotgun, took one last look at Joyce, pulled his camera out and snapped a photo of Veronica's body. He sprinted out the back door, dodging through the maze of alleys and side streets. He vanished into the night, leaving Joyce unconscious on the floor but relatively unharmed, a strange token of respect from a deeply twisted man.

He knew he had to vanish, to run far from this town and its ghosts. As he made his escape, the police found Joyce, who weakly called out for medical assistance.

Weeks turned into months, and Michael stayed one step ahead of the law. News outlets were buzzing with updates on the hunt for the notorious "Mailman Michael," linked now to a spree of disappearances.

In the depths of the night, as he drove on desolate roads, Michael listened to the radio, catching fragments of news reports about a Soldier who had killed himself because of a girl, a short blonde hair blue-eyed prostitute named Jendi.

A twisted smile played on his lips as he muttered to himself, "Maybe that's where I'm headed," he mused. He adjusted his rearview mirror, catching a glimpse of the dark road he'd left behind. Turning the steering wheel in his Ford Bronco he headed into the pitch-black night.

"I got this one" he whispered to himself, looking back at the dark road behind him.

"I'm mailman Michael".

The End.

ABOUT THE AUTHOR

Parvin Rosario, known as The Night Writer, is a visionary storyteller known for crafting thought-provoking narratives that explore the dark and often unsettling intersections of technology, society, and human nature.

With a background spanning 17 years in the US Military, a man of Puerto Rican origin and a childhood that raised him all throughout the east coast of America. Rosario's journey into the world of writing began during a deployment to Afghanistan. It was there, amidst the challenges and adventures, that Rosario's passion for storytelling took root. In the midst of missions in Afghanistan, Rosario penned his first complete story, "Juniors First Kill" a thrilling tale that would later become the foundation for his renowned series, "The Sol of Shadows". To his surprise and delight, the series quickly gained popularity throughout the Forward Operating Base, and Soldiers would ask Rosario for more of his nail bitting story's to past there time in the harsh conditions of war.

Drawing inspiration from his own life experiences and his time living abroad in Japan, Germany, and Poland, as well as his multiple combat tours in Iraq and Afghanistan, Rosario weaves intricate fantasy thrillers and sci-fi thrillers. His writing style is as dynamic as the stories he tells, with each thriller taking on a unique approach, filled with unexpected twists and mind-bending endings that leave readers yearning for more.

When you dive into a Night Writer novel, prepare to be transported to a realm where the lines between reality and imagination blur. With vivid descriptions, complex characters, and heart-stopping suspense, Rosario crafts stories that will make you feel as if you've stepped into a movie, living out the twists and turns alongside the characters. Parvin Rosario's upbringing has undoubtedly influenced his writing, infusing his work with a depth of emotion and an understanding of the human condition that resonates with readers. As he continues to captivate audiences with his imaginative storytelling, the Night Writer invites you to embark on a thrilling literary journey where reality and science fiction collide.

Nightwriter

Find your next story at

www.Nightwriter.one

Connect with the author

@NIGHTWRITER.ONE

Share your review with us!